TO DIE FOR

Kevin Norton and his friend are Russian agents about to go on a camper trip across Europe and western Asia, bringing support and money to terrorist cells. Their instructions are to take along a group of students, including Gemma and Marianne, as cover, with the ultimate aim of holding Gemma hostage. Gemma's father, a power player in D.C., is suspicious, and hires ex-CIA agent Ben Craig to keep an eye on the girls. Thus begins a long-distance war of nerves, pitting agent against agent, with Gemma's life as the prize . . .

Books by V. J. Banis
in the Linford Mystery Library:

THE WOLVES OF CRAYWOOD
THE GLASS PAINTING
WHITE JADE
DARKWATER
I AM ISABELLA
THE GLASS HOUSE
MOON GARDEN
THE SECOND HOUSE
ROSE POINT
THE DEVIL'S DANCE
SHADOWS
HOUSE OF FOOLS
FIVE GREEN MEN
THE SCENT OF HEATHER
THE BISHOP'S PALACE
BLOOD MOON
FIRE ON THE MOON
FATAL FLOWERS
THE LION'S GATE
TILL THE DAY I DIE
THE MYSTERY OF BLOODSTONE
PRISONER OF KELSEY HOUSE
THE MISTRESS OF EVIL
GHOST LAKE
MYSTERY OF THE RUBY
HAUNTED HELEN
THE MISSING MAN

V. J. BANIS

TO DIE FOR

Complete and Unabridged

LINFORD
Leicester

2019

First published in Great Britain

First Linford Edition
published 2019

*A catalogue record for this book is available
from the British Library.*

ISBN 978–1–4448–4202–9

Published by
F. A. Thorpe (Publishing)
Anstey, Leicestershire

Set by Words & Graphics Ltd.
Anstey, Leicestershire
Printed and bound in Great Britain by
T. J. International Ltd., Padstow, Cornwall

This book is printed on acid-free paper

1

He'd had to kill her.

'But you're the only one who knew,' she said. 'You're the only one I told.'

'Yes, that's true,' he confessed.

'But why?'

He wanted to say, 'Because it's what I do.' Instead, he said, 'One kiss, then. Please, one last kiss.'

And he had broken her neck. She must have known that was what he meant to do.

He'd been on his way to meet Ralph when she found him on the Strasse, accosted him, demanded that they talk. He left her lying on the floor of her apartment, took the stairs down to the vestibule, where he had left his bicycle, took it outside, and got on it.

They met in an old and no longer used cemetery on the outskirts of the German city of Hamburg. Because the cemetery was said to be haunted, no one else was likely to be there. Which made it, of course, the ideal place for a clandestine meeting.

Cemeteries held no fear for Kurt Reidl. It was the living who worried him more than the dead. Bridget had worried him, alive. But Bridget was dead now.

Ralph was already there when he arrived, riding his bike and leaving it in the deep shadows beneath an elm tree. He strolled to the mausoleum where they usually met. He saw the red tip of a cigarette before he saw Ralph.

They rarely bothered with conventional greetings. Time was always of the essence. 'The less time we spend together here,' as Ralph had one time explained it, 'the less danger there is of anyone seeing us.'

'The girl has been dealt with?' was his greeting on this occasion.

'Yes, I . . . ' He was going to say more, but Ralph held up a hand to forestall him.

'I don't need to know any details,' he said curtly. 'However, I think it wise for you to leave Germany for a time.'

'I'm going to Russia?' Kurt asked, delighted.

'In due time. For the present, you will be going to Paris.'

'Paris? But my French is not the best.'

'True, but your English is impeccable. Particularly your American English.'

'I am to be an American this time, then?'

'Exactly.' Ralph finished his cigarette and carefully pinched it out between his fingers, dropping the butt into the pocket of his jacket. He handed across a folded sheet of paper. 'You will meet up there with Ivan. His name now is Walter. Yours will be Kevin, Kevin Norton. Kurt Reidl must disappear.'

'Will I be staying in Paris?'

'Only briefly. You are going on a camper trip, during which time you will visit a number of our cells. He has the details. Oh, and there is a girl there in Paris, an American girl, Gemma Dolan. You will need to establish a relationship with her.'

By which, of course, he meant Kurt was to become her lover. 'What if she decides she does not like me?' he asked; and Ralph, who was never known to show

3

amusement, actually smiled at him. 'Like me in that way, I mean,' Kevin added, and smiled back.

'Dear boy,' Ralph had said, still smiling, 'then you will have to make her like you, will you not? In that way, I mean.'

★ ★ ★

The first time they saw Kevin Norton was at the newish Bastille Opera House, and not at the old barn, as they liked to call the Palais Gamier, though both of them knew perfectly well it was an exquisite building in perfect fin de siècle style. The opera being performed that evening was Richard Wagner's *The Flying Dutchman*, about a ghost ship and doomed mariners. The two young Americans, Gemma Dolan and her best friend Marianne Marker, had taken their seats just as the lights were dimming in the main auditorium, having lingered as long as they dared at the bar outside. Theirs were the expensive loge seats in the third row, the second and third seats in from the aisle;

and since the aisle seat was vacant, Gemma was about to suggest that they move one over, which would have given them a slightly better view of the stage, when the young man came in, hurrying down the aisle. He slipped into the empty seat next to Gemma at the very moment when the overture was starting, though the opera house rules, spelled out in the program, said quite clearly that if the music had begun you had to wait till the end of the first act before you could claim your seat.

Technically, of course, the music had not quite begun, surely at least not when he had come into the auditorium. Not to mention, he seemed to have no program to warn him of the rules. Anyway, you could hardly blame him for bending the rules a bit, as Gemma saw it: with Wagner, the first act could sometimes take forever, or at least so it often seemed to her. Wagner was not Gemma's favorite composer, but Marianne's parents back in the states had made a gift to their daughter of the tickets, and she had insisted Gemma come with her.

'I think what they had in mind when they sent you the tickets was that you might bring a date with you for the evening. As in a young man date,' Gemma had said when asked to come along, but Marianne had only scoffed at that suggestion.

'What difference does it make who I bring?' she asked. 'My parents won't even know, will they?'

'Parents always know, don't ask me how. Anyway, you know how they are,' Gemma replied. 'In their book, you've reached the old age of twenty-two, and you don't even have a boyfriend. They're probably wringing their hands and wondering if you're doomed to stay single the rest of your life. Even worse, they're probably convinced they'll never have grandchildren.'

'Actually, I think I kind of like the idea of staying single. Men can be such a hassle sometimes,' Marianne said with a laugh, but she quickly grew serious. 'Oh, I guess if I really put my mind to it, I could find someone in one of my classes to go out with. But you know as well as I do that we'll have more fun together, just the two of us. We always do, don't we?'

'Yes, that's true. But, Marianne,' Gemma said, making herself look and sound serious; she was actually a year younger than her friend, but it always felt like she was the older of the two.

'Here it comes,' Marianne said in mock dismay. 'The lecture from big sister. Big bossy sister.'

'Marianne,' Gemma started anew, undeterred, 'you've been here in Paris for nearly a year . . . '

'I know, I know,' Marianne said with a groan. 'And it'll all be over in two more weeks, my year abroad; after which it's back to Dayton, Ohio for me. And a job in a factory, probably one of those General Motors places. Dayton is a General Motors factory kind of town, if you didn't know.'

'Yes, I understand all that. What I actually started to say, though, was — '

'You've been here for a whole year and you haven't met any men yet,' Marianne finished for her in a mocking sing-song voice.

They both laughed, but Gemma quickly grew serious. 'Well it's true, isn't it?' she said. 'You've been in Paris for practically a year, apart from those two weeks. And you can't believe for a minute that your parents agreed to it just so that you could speak French and learn French history. They must've imagined a young Charles Boyer or some other continental lover sweeping you off your pretty feet, and so far you haven't been swept. You haven't met any men in that time. In Paris, the city of love. In a whole year.'

Marianne screwed up her face. 'No, that's not exactly true,' she said. 'I mean yes, it *is* the city of love; at least that's what they say. And, yes, I *have* met plenty of men — well, boys I suppose you'd have to call them; most of them don't come across as men. Not real men, not in my book. They're fellow students, mostly. And I'm not saying some of them aren't attractive — they are. Some of them are cute, seriously cute. Especially the Frenchies.'

'But . . . ?' Gemma raised a questioning eyebrow.

'But, they're French.' Marianne's voice

went up in something close to a wail. 'All of the cute ones are French.'

'Duh? We're in France, in Paris, going to school at the Sorbonne. So, yes, a lot of the guys you meet in class are likely to be French, don't you think? Frenchies, as you call them.'

'Don't be silly. You know what I mean,' Marianne said impatiently. 'You know how French men are, even the young ones. If a girl asks them out on a date, they have, well, they're going to have expectations.'

'Expectations? What expectations?'

'Expectations,' Marianne repeated firmly. 'They'd think the opera part was nothing but an excuse to get a girl into bed. Before the first act, so to speak. Talk about being swept off your feet. I'd be lucky to get out of the house with my clothes intact, all of them swept away, so to speak. At least if you go with me, I'll actually get to see the opera, which is more than I'd do with any of those guys. And I love *Dutchman*. I know you're not crazy about Wagner, but *Dutchman* is one of my favorites. So say yes, please; and if you go, I'll let you buy me a burger afterwards at that MacDonald's in the quarter. Where I took a solemn vow I'd never set foot.'

'God, your syntax is horrible. No wonder you've had such a struggle with the French language; you can't even manage good English.'

'*Bien sur*. Yes, but you knew exactly what I meant. Which is the whole point of grammar, isn't it? And I did vow never to go there, didn't I? But I will, I'll set foot — both feet, in fact — inside the place if you'll come to the opera with me.'

'And I get the privilege of buying you a burger after the opera?'

Marianne gave her a sly smile. 'If you pay for the burgers, I'll spring for a glass of bubbly during intermission.'

'Champagne? A whole glass? In that case, how can I refuse?'

It was a standing joke between them that Marianne was there on a scholarship and pinching every penny to keep herself afloat, and Gemma's father had 'bushels of money', as Marianne liked to put it.

'He's not rich,' Gemma often protested.

'My dad's a butcher,' Marianne pointed out. 'In comparison, yours is rich.'

'Plus he's hot,' Marianne had added more than once.

'Don't forget he's old, too,' Gemma said. 'He's forty-nine. Or, no, I think he was fifty on his last birthday. Yes, I'm sure. The card I sent had something funny about fifty on it. If I was wrong, I'd have heard about it by now.'

'Whatever. Age doesn't mean anything as far as I'm concerned. I mean, it's just a number, right? The point is, whatever his age, he's hot. To die for, if you ask me. Definitely to die for, for an older man. Not to mention there's something about that whole Washington power thing that curls a girl's toes. Power's so seductive.'

'In case you didn't know, right now he's unemployed. As a matter of fact, according to the last letter I got, they're off to the shore just now; North Carolina, I think. To get away from the Washington heat, I think Margaret said. And, yes, I mentioned my step-mother deliberately. He's married, you know.'

'I swear, sometimes it seems like all the good ones are married. Or gay. He's not gay, is he?'

'Hello? Would I be here if he was? If there's any man in the entire world I'd be willing to swear on a Bible doesn't have a single gay bone in his body, it'd be my father.'

'Hmm. I bet you're right, too. But you know what I mean. And not for long, either. Not for long unemployed, I mean, not the married part. They were hinting in the *Herald* just this morning that he might be the next secretary of state. Anyway, secretary or not, everybody knows he's a player. He has the president's ear. That's what the writer said in the *Herald* this morning: David Dolan has the president's ear. I can show you the actual line, on the front page, too. I marked it in red.'

'The president's ear?' Gemma made a face. 'Ugh. You make it sound like he ate it for breakfast. With maple syrup.'

'All I'm saying is that I'd let him bite mine off if that made him happy.'

'You don't mean happy, you mean horny.'

Marianne waggled a finger at her. 'Oh no, you know the rules. We don't talk about the sex stuff when discussing parents.'

'You're the one who started down that

track,' Gemma pointed out.

'Biting ears is not 'sex stuff'. Not technically. So never mind about all that anyway. The question is, will you come with me? To the opera? You haven't said yet. Pretty please?'

'Hmm.' Gemma pretended to hesitate, but they both knew she'd lost the argument. 'I suppose. But only if you let me buy us those burgers afterward.'

Marianne squealed with pleasure. 'With fries, the crisp greasy kind? And a Coke?'

'Check. With greasy fries and a Coke. Which, if I remember correctly, might be the best part of our meal. And I get a glass of bubbly during intermission.'

'Settled.'

So, of course, there they were at the opera. And Gemma, who was not looking forward to the music anyway, happened to glance to the side when the young man at the last minute slipped into the seat beside her; and for just the briefest of moments, a few seconds only, their eyes met.

And something electric went through her, so powerful that she very nearly cried aloud and rose from her seat.

2

It lasted for no more than second or two,
her ice-blue eyes and his mahogany-
brown ones (spaniel eyes, she liked to call
them) locked together; but the sensation
was so vivid she completely forgot about
the orchestra now blaring away in the
pit, forgot altogether that this was the
dreaded Wagner.

Plus, she was certain he had felt it too;
that shock of, well, she didn't know what
exactly it had been. It was like nothing
she had ever experienced before. She
chanced another glance and found him
totally absorbed in the music, completely
oblivious, it seemed, to the fact that she
was sitting beside him. Oblivious too, or
so he acted, to what had just happened
between them.

Which in itself was a new experience
for her. She knew perfectly well she was
pretty, or in any case that men found her
attractive, which was surely the same

thing. How could she not know this? Men had been making fools of themselves over her since she had been fourteen, just starting to fill out, with her blonde hair reaching to her shoulders then, though it was a bit shorter now.

And here, sitting mere inches away from her, was a man who did not even seem aware of her proximity. Who was completely ignoring her. Who seemed blithely unaware of her existence, in fact.

And the worst of it: he was, as Marianne would surely have put it, to die for.

* * *

Kevin Norton, the man sitting next to her, pretended not to notice that Gemma Dolan had given him another look. He kept his eyes fixed firmly on the stage below and the musicians sawing busily away in the pit. His assignment had been to start by gaining her trust, her friendship. If anything else developed, his instructions had been that he was to let it develop in its own time, not try to force it.

What exactly Ralph had in mind for her down the road, Kevin was not sanctioned to know, though he thought he had a pretty good idea. When the time came, Ralph would tell him whatever he needed to know.

Until then, since he was no fool, he knew perfectly well it was wisest to keep his mouth shut. That was how you got ahead in the party. Asking questions was only likely to get you into trouble. They were fanatic about the risk of betrayal. Everyone was suspect, especially anyone who showed too much curiosity, anyone who asked too many questions.

Keep your mouth shut, and do as you were told. That was the key to success.

And what he had been told in this instance was to establish a relationship with this girl. Period.

'But,' Ralph had said, that night in the German cemetery, and his smile had vanished as quickly as it had come, 'this Gemma Dolan, she is important, but only of secondary importance. Nothing must interfere with your assignment.'

★　★　★

Before the music had even begun, in that time of milling crowds and excited anticipation, he had spent about half an hour in the lobby, observing the two young women without their knowing it. He had already pegged Marianne as the more vulnerable of the two. She was not unattractive, though next to her companion she looked drab indeed. He suspected she spent much of her time, probably too much of it, in the shadow of her luminous friend.

Yes, luminous was a good word for Gemma Dolan. Certainly she was beautiful. And he was almost equally certain that she was aware of her beauty. She looked to him the type who was all too conscious of the reactions of men to her good looks, reactions that she actually scorned, though she was almost certainly adept as well at not letting men know that.

These observations, then, had decided for him how he would play it with her. He would arouse her curiosity, disarm her.

He would make her think his intentions were entirely innocent, let her believe that he had no interest in romancing her. That approach was almost sure to pique her interest.

Which was why, when the first act ended, he remained sitting and contrived to have, not Gemma, but her friend, step on his foot as they struggled to make their way past him. Heartfelt apologies followed from Miss Marianne Marker (yes, he knew her name also, practically everything there was to know about her; about both of them, in fact; he had come, as he always did, well prepared) while Gemma waited in the aisle, looking bored. For his part, he had brushed the incident off as of no consequence.

'Really it was my fault, having my big feet in the way,' he assured Marianne, suppressing the temptation to laugh, because the statement was truer than she would ever have imagined. He had managed to put his foot in the way at exactly the right moment for the desired result. What had seemed to her like an accident, her accident, had been a carefully planned move on his part, a means of making himself recognizable to her.

What he knew by that time, though, was that this assignment was going to be harder than he had expected. The Dolan girl was right in thinking he had felt that electric jolt between them for those few seconds when their eyes had happened to meet. He had not been expecting that.

He was used to handling women, and he was as every bit as aware of his good looks and his sexual attractiveness as she was of hers. It was why his assignments had more often than not involved the seducing of one young woman or another. Often they were the plain Janes, the overweight ones, sometimes even the disabled. 'Broken sparrows', he sometimes called them. The ones not used to having a handsome young man focus his sexual energies on them. It was simple, even laughingly simple in his mind, to get them into bed; and once he convinced them that he was in love, that this was the reason he had wanted them so desperately, why then they almost invariably fell in love with him as well.

His success was rarely even in question. And once they were in love with him, there was almost no secret they would not gladly share with him. And for this he actually got paid. It was pleasant enough work, as he saw it. He had always found the old adage to be true: 'In the dark . . . ' All was well, so long as he did not let himself take any of them seriously. And up till now, that had not happened. They had, every one of them, been nothing more than trophies, notches on his belt, if you wanted to think of them that way. Which was how, in fact, he did think of them.

But his every instinct was warning him now to be careful with this one, with Gemma Dolan; that she was likely to be different.

And yes, I can do that, Kevin told himself, keeping his eyes carefully and rigidly forward. Indeed, it promised to be a very enjoyable assignment, if not without certain unexpected risks, risks he had never faced before.

If only it were not for this interminable music, he was thinking. He loathed opera, Wagner most of all.

3

By the time the house lights had gone down and the instruments in the pit had begun playing the music for Act Two, it was clear from his empty seat that the young man who had been sitting next to them was not coming back.

'He must've vanished during the intermission,' Gemma said in a whisper. She found herself wishing she'd done the same. She had a fleeting vision of the two of them dashing into the Paris night together. But it seemed after all that he had not shared whatever her strange experience had been, that moment when their eyes had locked together, however briefly. She would have sworn otherwise, though.

Throughout the entire intermission, she had fully expected him to take advantage of the incident with Marianne to come talk to them, to offer further apologies. It was the kind of thing men routinely did; they looked for any opportunity to strike up an acquaintance with her, and took advantage of whatever presented itself. She had long since grown used to it. And in her mind, the young man had created a perfect opportunity for himself. Or perhaps Marianne had created it for him.

So she had already made up her mind that when he did show up, as she was convinced he would, to offer his apologies once again and introduce himself, she would be cool and aloof, to let him know that she was not interested in getting better acquainted.

'I felt like such an idiot,' Marianne insisted for the umpteenth time during that intermission. 'He must have thought that I'm a real klutz.' They were in the bar area just then, having that glass of champagne Marianne had promised beforehand.

'I wouldn't worry too much about it, if I was you,' Gemma told her. 'I don't think he minded much. And it wasn't like you left him crippled or anything.'

Marianne laughed. 'Yes, I think he'll live to walk again. But he was to die for, don't you think?'

'He was nice-looking, yes,' Gemma agreed. 'And I think when we see him again, he'll totally brush off the foot incident. I bet our next encounter will happen before we even get back to our seats for Act Two.'

'Do you really think so?' Marianne's eyes sparkled with anticipation. 'What makes you say that?'

'I know men,' Gemma said drily.

'Better than I do, that's for sure.' Marianne looked around the crowded lobby. 'But I don't see him anywhere. And there's the warning bell for the next act. Should we go back inside? Or do you think he'll still show up here?'

'I think he knows full well where to find us.' Gemma emptied her champagne glass and set it atop the bar with a loud *thunk*, earning her a look from the bartender that started out angry and softened considerably once he had gotten a good look at her.

But the handsome young stranger had not found them, in or out of the auditorium, as it happened; and from the look of the empty seat next to Gemma's, he was not intending to either. Which left her feeling strangely annoyed, although she could not have articulated to herself just why that should be so. She made a determined effort to put the young man out of her mind and concentrate instead upon the music. But the music did nothing to brighten her mood. It was Wagner, after all.

★   ★   ★

Nor did the business at lunch the next day make her mood any brighter. The two friends ordinarily had lunch together at a small café not far from the university, and since Gemma was free of classes from midmorning on, and Marianne had French history just before lunch, Gemma was always the first to arrive at the café.

So it was on the morning after the opera. Gemma was already at their usual table, enjoying a cup of coffee while she waited. And when Marianne did finally show up to join her, who should she have in tow but the very same young man from the night before. Gemma recognized him at once, even from half a block away.

'Kevin Norton, Gemma Dolan,' Marianne introduced them, and added, in a rush of words, to Gemma, 'We bumped into each other after history class, and it turns out he's American, too, and he doesn't know anyone here, and he's feeling as much of a fish out of water as we did our first few days. You remember what that was like, how horrible it was. Strangers in a strange land. So I invited him to join us for lunch. You don't mind, do you?'

'No, of course not,' Gemma said, but in a cool voice. She extended her hand. He took it and held it just a second or two longer than might have been quite necessary. 'But am I the only one,' she asked, 'who thinks it's kind of a coincidence, you bumping into each other like that, after sitting together last night?'

'Just for Act One,' Marianne said. 'And I know it might look that way, but it isn't. It turns out we're in the same class, French history, so it was practically inevitable that we'd run into each other sooner or later.'

'Then I'm surprised you didn't recognize each other last night,' Gemma said, 'if you're taking a class together. You must've seen each other lots of times before.'

'Oh, that's easily explained,' he answered for Marianne. 'I'm not actually taking that class, so this was the first time today that I was there. I was auditing the class, actually, to see if I thought it was going to be my cup of tea.' He gave Gemma the benefit of a big grin.

'And of course you decided it is,' she said, returning his smile with a skeptical one to let him know she was on to his game.

'As a matter of fact, I decided it isn't for me,' he said, making a face. 'All those French kings. Charles this one, and Charles that one, and Francis and Louie, and blah blah blah. I'm not very good with names. I'm sure I'd never get them straight.'

Marianne gave a bark of a laugh. 'Oh, if you only knew,' she said. 'I've gotten real headaches trying to memorize them, and I still don't know if I'll pass the course.'

The two of them laughed at that.

'So what are you taking, then,' Marianne asked when the laughter had faded, 'if not French history? Literature? I have that class too.'

He gave a shrug. 'I don't know yet. I haven't decided. Maybe nothing. It was just an idea I had, of enrolling in some classes while I'm here in Paris.'

'You're just passing through, then?' Marianne asked.

Another shrug. 'I've got a friend, Walter — he goes by Walt — who's living here in Paris. I came to visit him, which is why I'm here. And now he's trying to convince me to go on a trip with him. You know, the open road, the romantic adventure. He's got a camper and is looking for some people to join him. Ideally, he'd like to enlist some students for the trip. And well, I'm thinking seriously about joining him.'

'Join him where?' Gemma asked. She was thinking, *Didn't we just hear he knew nobody here?*

'I doubt if Walt even knows himself where he's going,' Kevin said. 'Not all of it, anyway. As I understand it, he plans to start in Amsterdam. Well, here, of course, but from here he'll be going to Amsterdam, where they'll do some work on the camper, to make it more suitable for a long haul with a group of travelers. And then he sets out from Amsterdam to . . . well, I don't think it's all been carved in stone yet. I think he's planning on India eventually. Delhi, I think he said. Between here and there . . . ?' Another of those shrugs. Which struck Gemma as more Gallic than American; or, hmm, she wasn't sure. Slavic, maybe. Didn't eastern Europeans shrug a lot?

'Walt is sort of the footloose and fancy-free type, if you know what I mean,' Kevin added. 'Which explains a lot, I guess.'

Marianne gave an eloquent sigh. 'It sounds wonderful to me,' she said. 'Footloose and fancy-free. Hitting the open road, just rambling around, seeing some of the world before I have to go back to my mundane life in Ohio.'

'Like I say, Walt's looking for some people to join him,' Kevin said quickly. 'I could link you up with him, if you're interested.' His eyes included Gemma in the offer.

'I don't know. It sounds expensive,' Marianne said hesitantly.

'I don't think he's exactly planning anything luxurious,' Kevin said. 'Everyone would be kind of roughing it. You know, out-of-the way places — hostels, campsites, that kind of thing. You shouldn't expect anything fancy. Anyway, as it happens, I have a little extra cash right now. I could front you, if that's a problem.'

'So you've got an income and everything?' Gemma asked.

'Not really. But I have an uncle, Ralph; he's got plenty of money, and I'm his favorite nephew, so he's generous sometimes. Which is why I've got enough to make the offer.'

'That's really nice of you, especially since we've only just met,' Gemma said. 'But Marianne knows I'm good for the money.' She did not add in so many words, but the implication was certainly there: *The two of us, Marianne and I, have not just met.*

'Thanks, both of you, but I'm not interested in being anyone's charity case,' Marianne said. After a few seconds, however, her disappointed expression brightened. 'But now that I think of it, I did just get some money from my folks, to buy my plane ticket home. I suppose they would just have sent the ticket, but for some reason they think tickets are cheaper here. Anyway, I guess I could use that money, or some of it. But, Gemma . . . ' She gave her friend a look of appeal. 'I couldn't do it on my own. I just couldn't. You know how I am. I'd be too scared.'

'You wouldn't be alone,' Kevin said. 'Or even the only girl on the trip. As I understand it, Walt's planning on maybe three girls, and four or maybe five boys. So even if your friend says no, you could still be part of a group.'

Gemma gave him a dubious look. 'Sorry if I sound a little cynical, but I can't help wondering what kind of plans he has for the girls.'

Kevin had the good grace to blush. 'Not *that*,' he said quickly. 'The girls will sleep in the camper; he plans to install berths for them. That's part of what they'll be doing in Amsterdam. But three berths are about as many as the van could accommodate comfortably, so the girls will use them and sleep inside, and the guys will be outside. They've all been told to bring a sleeping bag.'

'That sounds reasonable,' Marianne said. 'If the guys don't mind.'

'But,' Kevin went on, giving her a gracious smile, 'I have to warn you, since word's gotten around about his plans, he's been overrun by students wanting him to pick them for the trip. It seems like everyone wants to get into the act. And I can't say I really blame them. It's the chance of a lifetime, isn't it?'

'So it doesn't sound as if he needs us,' Gemma said, 'if there are already so many volunteers.'

'Oh, I'm sure if I put in a good word for the two of you, there'll be no problem with your making the cut. But he'll want to meet you, of course, before he decides. And I wouldn't wait too long to make your minds up. Like I said, a lot of kids already have their hands in the air. I was surprised by the response.'

'Gemma?' Marianne said, giving her friend another pleading look. 'What do you say?'

'I'll have to think about it,' Gemma said.

'I wouldn't . . . ' Kevin started to say.

'I know,' she cut him off, 'you wouldn't take too long.' She was thinking that Marianne was already half smitten with this stranger. *And if he even once gave her the looks he's been giving me since they arrived, like a hungry dog eyeing a steak on the table, well, Marianne would be a goner for sure.*

She did not in fact think Kevin actually had any interest in Marianne, but if the two of them were alone, more or less, in a camper, for weeks upon weeks, that could easily enough change. Kevin Norton did not impress her as a young man who cared for abstinence on any score. And Marianne was indeed vulnerable where men were concerned, an attractive girl who somehow thought of herself as a plain Jane.

33

'Look,' Gemma said aloud with a sigh of resignation, 'my last class today gets out at three thirty. What if we go to meet your friend then, say, at four o'clock?'

Kevin looked inordinately pleased. 'I'll set it up for four this afternoon.'

'In the parking lot just outside the cafeteria?'

'Got it.'

'Then, if your friend decides he approves of us . . . '

'I'm sure he will, if I tell him it's all right,' Kevin said with another big grin. 'He generally takes my advice on things like that.'

Gemma nodded. 'I'm glad to hear it. And if he does, say this afternoon, decide he wants to include us, that'll still give me plenty of time to write to my father this evening, to let him know our plans. That's if we end up *having* plans. He was expecting me to come home once school let out.'

Kevin gave her a scornful look. 'Still tied to Daddy's apron strings, are we?' he asked in a scathing tone.

'Not that it's any of your business, but

it's more his purse strings. He's financing my time abroad. Which, by the way, brings up another question I'll need an answer for. He'll be sending me a check soon. My allowance, if you want to know. Footloose and fancy-free is fine, but there are still always expenses to account for. Meaning, I'll have to tell him where to send the check. Any suggestions?'

Kevin thought a moment. 'Well, after Amsterdam we're going to Brussels, but I don't think Walt plans on staying there long. So it's possible we might be gone before his check gets there.'

'And after Brussels?' Gemma paused to study a map of Europe in her head. 'If he's heading for India, he probably plans to travel through Germany, right? So I could tell my father to send it to Munich, maybe?'

'No,' Kevin said a little too quickly, too emphatically. Both girls gave him puzzled looks. 'It's just that I don't speak any German,' he said hurriedly. 'And I'm sure Walt doesn't know any either. What about the two of you?'

He could not very well tell them that

thanks to some recent activities in which he had been engaged there, Germany was not a safe destination for him at present. It was entirely possible that the German police even had a warrant out for him. Certainly he did not want to find out. It was safer for him to avoid that country if he could.

Gemma and Marianne both shook their heads at his question. 'I speak a word or two, but nothing more than the basic stuff,' Gemma said. '*Bitte, danke, Guten Tag*. The usual. Nothing complicated.'

'I don't even know that much,' Marianne said. 'Not a word.'

'Well, then, there you have it,' Kevin said. He looked, Gemma thought, a bit too relieved. 'Germany is out. We don't want to find ourselves someplace where we can't even order food.'

'But didn't you mention India?' Gemma raised an eyebrow. 'How would we order food there? I don't even know what they speak in India.'

'English,' Kevin said, and when she looked doubtful, he added, 'The Raj, remember. The British were there forever.

They hate the British, but everyone in India speaks English. At least, so I've heard.'

'Well, where then?' Gemma asked. 'If not Germany, where should I tell Daddy we'll be?'

'I know Walt plans on getting to Istanbul eventually.'

'Istanbul?' Gemma's eyebrows shot up. 'That's clear across Europe from here. It'll take weeks to get there. Unless that camper's rocket-powered.' And, she thought, surely everyone in Turkey didn't speak English either.

'I'll tell you what,' Kevin said, brightening. 'I've always wanted to see Italy. If we headed south from Brussels, we could cut through Switzerland, and probably a corner or two of France, and we'd be on the road to Italy. And from there, we could take a ferry from southern Italy to Greece. I'm pretty sure they run those ferries regularly.'

'Greece?' Marianne took on a dreamy look.

'We might as well see all the ancient civilizations while we're at it,' Kevin said.

'I'd love to see Italy,' Marianne said. 'And Greece. But what will your friend say? About going that way, I mean. He must already have an itinerary planned, even if it's just in his head.'

'In that case, we'd just have to persuade him to see Italy. So, then,' he said to Gemma, 'have Daddy send whatever to Rome, care of American Express. We should be there in about a week and a half, by my calculation. Maybe two weeks; but American Express will hold it if we're a little late. And that way we can skip Germany completely.'

But there will be others besides the three of us on the trip, Gemma found herself thinking. *How do we know one of them might not be fluent in German?*

'Then you'll go?' Marianne asked Gemma.

'We'll see,' Gemma replied, but of course both of them knew the fight was over. 'We still have to meet Walt, who might just think we're both obnoxious.'

'I doubt that,' Kevin said.

'And, frankly,' Gemma added, 'if I'm going to be living in it for months, I want to see this camper, too.'

'Well . . . ' Kevin hesitated. 'It won't exactly be fitted out yet. That'll happen in Amsterdam.'

'Then he can tell me what he's planning,' she said. 'And show me. I have a pretty good imagination.'

So I see, he was thinking, but he only gave her a smile. 'I'm sure he'll be happy to,' he said.

4

They met Walt after Gemma's last class, in the parking lot nearest to the cafeteria. He was patient in answering all of Gemma's questions.

'I hear there'll be berths inside for the girls to sleep in,' Gemma said. 'Can you show me?'

'Well, the berths aren't there yet,' he said. 'I'm having those installed in Amsterdam, along with some other modifications. But I can show you where they'll be, if you want.'

'I *do* want,' she told him.

'Sure.' He took her inside the camper. 'Just here, around the windows,' he said, slapping the side of the van with the palm of his hand. 'I say around the windows, but I really mean above and below the windows. And only three, because that way the windows will still open and close. We'll probably have some warm weather where we're headed, so I'm having air conditioning put in while we're in Amsterdam, but it'll save on fuel if we can open the windows some of the time.'

'And the men will be sleeping outside?'

'Absolutely. You ladies will have the van to yourselves at night. If you're nervous, you can even lock yourselves in.'

When he met the girls and was showing them the camper, Walt was enthusiastic about their joining his trek. 'Maybe we'll even go around the world. I'm not ruling anything out. Of course, if anyone else has a suggestion, I'm all ears,' he told them. 'And needless to say, but I'll say it anyway — it'd be great to have you along. Both of you.' This was said with warm smiles all around.

Later, however, when he was alone with Kevin, he expressed quite a different opinion. 'You must be out of your mind,' he said angrily, slipping without even thinking about it into Russian. 'Those girls are too smart. The pretty one is, for sure. She will figure things out long before we even get to India.'

'Speak English. We are Americans now, remember,' Kevin said sharply. 'And as for those two girls, this is not optional for us. Gemma Dolan is important, important to Ralph, certainly.' He added, 'And the other one, Marianne, is her friend. They do everything together. Which makes her important too.'

'Everything?' Walt switched to English as well and gave him a lascivious look.

'Don't even think about it,' Kevin warned him. 'At the end of our journey, we are to deliver Miss Dolan unharmed to Ralph, in America. That is all we need to know, for now anyway. And, yes, she is the pretty one, the blonde, if you are wondering. The prettiest one, anyway. I think they are both attractive.'

'Both of them are bright, too. But Miss Dolan is the brightest one, it seems to me,' Walt said. 'Frankly, she's also the one who scares me the most.' He hesitated before saying, 'Did you know she took pictures of the license plates? On the camper, when I was showing her around?'

'Did she?' Kevin was startled by this news.

'At least I'm pretty sure she did,' Walt corrected himself. 'She was photographing everything inside and out. With her cell phone, if you didn't notice. Snap, snap, snap, never stopping.'

Kevin snorted. 'You're the technician. That's the kind of thing you are supposed to notice.'

'I did notice. That's why I am telling you about it now. She took pictures of the outside of the camper, from every possible angle. Some of them must show the plates.'

Kevin let out the big breath he had taken. 'Only coincidentally, then, I'd say. Look, stop worrying about Gemma Dolan. I will handle her.'

'The same way you handled Bridget?' Walt asked.

'Do not even mention that name,' Kevin said sternly. 'You are supposed to have forgotten about that. We both are. And, no, Gemma Dolan is more valuable to us alive than dead, thank you. And that's as much as you need to know on that subject.'

'Dolan? Dolan?' Walt screwed up his face thoughtfully. 'Wait, her father isn't . . . '

'Enough! You know as well as I do, asking questions is sometimes not good for one's health. She is going with us, and that's that, everything you need to know. As much as either of us needs to know. Don't be a fool.'

Walt nodded his understanding, but he was smiling. *Well, well,* he thought, *David Dolan's daughter, and entrusted to our care for months. Talk about an opportunity.*

* * *

Ben Craig paused in the foyer of the Smithsonian and looked around. Yes — there, only a few feet inside the doors, as his instructions had said, was a man in a gray trench coat looking carefully away but holding a *Time* magazine under his arm, so that the front cover was plain to see. Just as Craig had been told.

The man with the magazine must have seen Ben come through the doors, however, because he started almost at once walking slowly in the direction of the dinosaur exhibit. Ben followed at a reasonable distance, pausing now and then to look around, ostensibly at various exhibits, but in fact to see if by any chance there was anyone following him. There was not. Had there been, he would almost certainly have detected them. On that score, he was practically infallible.

The man he was following had entered the dinosaur exhibit and stopped by a brass rail. Ben walked closer and stopped alongside the same rail. Like his contact, he seemed to be admiring the enormous skeleton before them.

'Impressive, isn't it?' the man with the magazine said.

'It always reminds me of what little creatures we are,' Ben replied.

'And yet, like that one, we can be deadly.'

'Maybe the deadliest of all,' Ben agreed.

In a much lower voice, the stranger said, 'I accidentally dropped a package, just there, by my feet. No, don't pick it up now. Wait until I've gone. You can find it then and seem to come looking for me, to return it. You'll be the proverbial good Samaritan. No one will even notice when you leave the building with the package under your coat.'

The stranger had turned his head slightly when he said this. Ben blinked his eyes at what he had seen. 'Yes, Mister . . . ' He started to say, 'Mister Dolan,' and checked himself. The stranger had at no time given him a name, which almost certainly meant that he intended to remain anonymous. Ben had been in the business long enough to know when to keep his mouth shut. If David Dolan did not wish to be recognized, then he would not be.

'Everything I need is in the package?' he asked instead.

'Everything. There are pictures of the girls . . . '

'I'm supposed to get them away, is that right?'

'No, no,' the stranger said quickly in a hoarse whisper. 'Not unless you think they're in any kind of danger. Mostly you just need to keep an eye on them. Probably it'd be best if you struck up a friendship with one or the other, or even both, just in case. But you're the operative. I'll leave the details entirely in your hands. You come highly recommended, by the way. I'm told you're very capable.'

Meaning, Ben thought, *he knows I was almost twenty years with the CIA. And if he knows that much, then he knows the rest of it, too. Including why I was fired. And most likely, he also knows that I've dried out since then. Or he probably wouldn't have arranged this meeting.*

'Is there contact information in the package?' he asked. 'Just in case I have any questions or problems?'

'Everything's there that you could possibly need. Including my name. Not my real one, of course — we both know how that works — but it'll do. And a phone number, and an email address. You can reach me at either. There are pictures of the van, too, and of its plates, so you shouldn't have any trouble identifying that. The van and its occupants were on their way to Italy by way of Amsterdam, according to the latest information I've had, but it should be easy to catch up with them. In fact, as far as I know, they're still in Amsterdam, where the camper's being retrofitted for the trip. If you leave in the next day or two, you'll probably find them there. There's plenty of money in the package — cash, enough for your travel expenses and your fees; but if you need more, contact me. This is important, and I don't want any slip-ups for any reason. Money least of all.'

'Tell me about the men, the ones the girls are traveling with. Have they been identified?'

'There's a picture of them — of the whole group — in the package too. There are seven of them altogether. Another girl, who's French I think, and four young men. The French girl and the Italian and the Swedish men probably aren't important; but the two in charge are on the left end of the group, and they're the ones you need to be interested in. The one in the plaid shirt, with the beard, his name's Walt Prescott. It's his camper, apparently. The other one, with brown hair and to Prescott's right, wearing a blue turtleneck, goes by the name of Kevin. Kevin Norton.'

'He "goes by the name of"? Do you have reason to think that's not his real name?' Walt asked.

'Let's just say I think there's something

fishy about him. He went to Columbia, he says, where he allegedly took some journalism courses. He says he intends to become a journalist.'

'Let me guess: there's no record of him at Columbia?'

'There is a record of a Kevin Norton, yes. But the physical description I have of him doesn't match that photo.' In fact, though David Dolan did not say so, the description he had been given (short, fat, florid complexion, with thin blond hair but prematurely balding) was in no way even remotely similar to the young man in the photo. That was what had first raised his suspicions, and led to this meeting.

'And the other one?' Craig asked.

'Walter Prescott?' Dolan chuckled under his breath. 'That guy seems to have sprung up fully formed, like Minerva. Do you know that story? The Greeks were so wonderfully inventive. It seems Zeus had a terrible headache one day, so to accommodate him his wife cut his head open with an axe, and out jumped Minerva in full battle gear, armor and all.'

'And our Walter wears armor?' Ben asked, puzzled.

'Maybe, in a sense. But, no, at least not the metallic kind. What I meant was, he doesn't seem to have any more antecedents than Minerva did. And now, Mr. Craig, I want a promise from you. I want you to promise me that no matter what happens, you won't tell my daughter about this meeting.'

'I do, sir. I promise.' Craig kept his face expressionless and stifled the smile that threatened. David Dolan had just blown his cover. Intentionally, or not? It was hard to say, but he doubted that David Dolan did very much by accident.

'Then goodbye, Mister Craig. Contact me if you need anything. Money, information, whatever, just let me know. And, needless to say, but I'll say it anyway — if anything comes out about this in the media, I'll deny any knowledge of you or this meeting. And wait, please, until I'm gone before you realize I've lost my package and try to return it to me.'

★   ★   ★

Ben Craig did see the girls and their companions in Amsterdam, where they were marking time while the camper was outfitted for them. (And did they know, any of them, that the garage where the work was being done was Russian-owned? he wondered. Certainly Walt Prescott and Kevin Norton must have known, though the others remained ignorant, it seemed.)

Then, suddenly, they had disappeared. One day the two young women were strolling alongside one of the canals, unaware of him strolling far behind them, just close enough to keep them in sight; and the next day they were gone, van and everyone.

5

'But we can't see Rome in just one day,' Gemma argued.

'I'm sorry to have to tell you,' Kevin said, and he did sound genuinely sorry, 'but we're not going to 'see' Rome at all, apart from the American Express office, and we'll only be there long enough to pick up your letter from Daddy.'

They had left the others back at the campsite, which was well outside the city. Kevin and Gemma had ridden into town on a borrowed scooter. She had thought, at least, that the two of them would be able to do some sight-seeing when they arrived, and though she was sorry everyone else had to miss 'The Eternal City', she was looking forward to a day or so exploring it.

'But that's ridiculous,' she said. They had stopped along the way for coffee at a roadside stand. 'Are you telling me we're just zooming there to get my letter, and straight back to the boondocks?'

''Fraid so. The fees for that campsite are pretty steep, so Walt's decided as soon as the two of us get back, we're going to hit the road again.'

'But that campsite is miles from anywhere,' Gemma protested. 'How can it possibly be expensive?'

'This is Italy,' he said. 'And it's summer, the height of the tourist season. Everything's expensive.'

'Look,' she said after a moment's thought, 'I still have money from my last check. For god's sake, I've hardly spent anything so far. How could I? We haven't been anywhere but those out-of-the-way camping places. What if I treat the two of us to hotel rooms for, say, even one night? We couldn't exactly hit the town, but we'd have time to see at least a few of the local sights.'

'And if Walt just goes and leaves us behind?' he asked. 'What then?'

'Then I guess we'd go back to Paris, and to hell with him. I'm tired of being dictated to.'

'Besides, it wouldn't be fair to the

others, would it? I mean, you and me playing tourists while they sit back there in the van, twiddling their thumbs?'

'I think I've done my fair share of thumb-twiddling,' she said. 'All the way here, to tell you the truth. We haven't seen or done anything except drive.'

'That's what you do when you travel by camper. You drive, or you ride,' he said. 'And as for seeing nothing, we've just come through the Swiss Alps. You can't say they weren't impressive. We even drove past Mt. Blanc.'

'Sure, impressive. But I would've liked to be impressed by some of the Swiss cities, too. Bern, or Zurich or, I don't know, St. Moritz.'

'That's so like you,' he said. 'St. Moritz, the playground of the rich.'

'I doubt everyone who goes there is rich. And besides, even if it was expensive — '

'It is.'

' — we could've gone there for lunch, or a glass of wine or something. But we didn't get within a hundred miles of the place. Or anyplace interesting. For that matter, isn't there a train that goes up Mt. Blanc? Or up the Alps, anyway? A nice, clean, efficient Swiss train. That couldn't be too expensive for anyone.'

'You're talking like a spoiled American kid,' Kevin said, putting his helmet back on and walking back to their scooter. 'You knew before we even started out that everyone in the group was pinching pennies. Including your friend, Marianne. Walt made a commitment to all of them, to try to save money for them when he can. And, yes, that often means staying in out-of-the-way places.'

'And he hasn't made a commitment to me, is that what you're saying?'

'You're the only one with a rich father,' he said, straddling the scooter. 'Come on, get on. We've got to move if we're going to get there and be back before it gets dark, and the guy who loaned me this said the lights aren't very good for night driving.'

Gemma put on her own helmet and got on the scooter behind him. But she felt as if he had just dismissed her objections out of hand. This was not the trip that she had been expecting when she agreed to come along.

She put her arms around him and held on as he raced onto the autostrada and merged with the fast-moving traffic, a river of cars, all of them rushing toward Roma — sixty kilometers ahead, as an overhead sign informed her.

Roma? One of the world's great cities? And all she was going to see was the inside of an American Express office?

She felt cheated.

★　★　★

Despite the photos and the detailed descriptions (of the camper, its license plates, its passengers, even their intended route), Ben Craig did not again cross paths with Gemma and her companions until they had reached Florence, and then it happened only by the merest chance.

He was having lunch in the Piazza della Signoria when he suddenly realized that those two pretty girls two tables over were the very ones he had seen in Amsterdam and had been searching for since then.

To be sure, they had changed their hair. Both of them had cut it short, presumably because it was easier to manage while traveling. They wore almost no makeup now, and their smart Paris outfits had been swapped for some plain-looking drip-dry pieces; but it was indeed the same two young ladies. He stared at them over the rim of his coffee cup.

He thought, as he had when he had seen her in Amsterdam — though that had only been at a considerable distance, that the pictures he had first seen of her back in Washington had failed to do Gemma Dolan justice. She was, literally, breathtaking, and neither a lack of makeup nor the change to cheap clothing could disguise that fact. But it was not her looks alone that made her stand out the way she did. There were plenty of good-looking young women in the world. What she had was that extra spark, that indefinable something that made some women staggeringly beautiful, and others, some of them even just as pretty, simply ordinary.

But now that he had found them again,

these two for whom he had been searching, what was he to do about it? He could not very well just stroll over to their table and start talking, though he suspected that more than a few men over the years had tried that very ploy.

And whatever he meant to do, it would have to be done quickly. It was evident at a glance that the two young ladies had finished their lunches; and now, gathering up a few parcels and what was obviously a guide book, they stood up, preparing to leave.

That was when Gemma Dolan's companion, Marianne Marker, gave him the very opportunity he had been seeking. She left her purse on the ground, by the leg of her chair, and started to walk away without it.

'Signorina, wait,' he called after them in Italian. 'You forgot your . . . ' He struggled for the word. Damn, how had his Italian gotten so rusty? He had used to speak it fluently. 'Your borsa. Yes, that's it. You forgot your borsa. Your bag.' He gesticulated, pointing at the errant purse.

The two young women laughed. 'Oh,

my purse. I'm such an idiot,' Marianne said with a squeal, and ran back to where she had left it. 'Thanks a lot — I'd have been in serious trouble if I'd left it behind. It's got everything in it. My money, my passport — well, everything.'

'But you didn't need to struggle for the Italian words,' the blonde one, the pretty one (Gemma Dolan, he reminded himself) said. 'We're not Italian. We're American, both of us. The same as you, I'd say, if I had to make a guess.'

He gave her a sheepish grin. 'Well, I was trying to act like a native, but words failed me. It happens a lot,' he said. 'But it was easier and less embarrassing trying to think what to yell than trying to run after you carrying a purse.'

The two young women laughed with him at that image. 'But,' he said, looking desperate, 'you really are American? In that case, please, I beg you, take pity on a lonely traveler. *Je suis desolate . . .* '

'*Désolé*' Gemma said. 'You mean, *je suis désolé.* You're sorry. Or I suppose it can mean you're desperate.'

'Well, I certainly am,' Ben said.

'Desperate. And sorry too, I suppose. I haven't talked to a fellow American in weeks. Let me buy you a drink, or coffee, or whatever. Anything, just to get you to sit and talk with me. Five minutes, that's all I ask. If you say no, if I hear one more word of Italian in the next five minutes, I swear to you on all that's holy, I'm going to slit my wrists.'

'Well,' Marianne said, giving her friend a questioning look, 'if you put it like that, how can we refuse?'

'Besides, I'd rather not have your death on our hands,' Gemma said, starting back toward the café where they had earlier eaten lunch. 'Anyway, like they say, you only live once.'

'Great,' Ben said. He introduced himself and ordered two glasses of red wine (what they had been drinking earlier when he had spotted them having lunch; thank god they hadn't noticed him) and a coffee for himself. 'But what you said suggests you think you're taking a risk by being here with me. Please tell me I'm not going to have angry parents swooping down on me accusing me of messing around with their lovely daughters.'

The girls laughed at that suggestion; laughter seemed to come easily to both of them, he noted. 'No parents, no,' Marianne said. 'They're oceans away.'

'Just friends,' Gemma said. 'But *they* might come swooping down on us. We've kind of gone AWOL.'

'From . . . ?' He shook his head. 'I'm confused. And when you say 'friends,' do you mean, like, boyfriends? Because I'd rather not have to fight a couple of angry guys.' He laughed.

'Just friends,' Gemma said emphatically. 'Though I think someone would like to believe it's more than that.'

'So, then, you said you've gone AWOL. What's that all about?' The wines and his coffee came at that moment. He slipped the waiter enough to cover the drinks and a generous tip, guaranteeing they could sit as long as they liked and they would not be interrupted. At least, not by the waiter.

'Can you believe,' Marianne said, 'we came here by camper, all the way from Amsterdam, and we haven't even seen a city yet? Before this one, I mean.'

'Just campsites,' Gemma said.

'Really remote ones,' Marianne added. 'But *you* got to see Rome,' she pointed out.

Gemma snorted. 'From the back of a scooter. And all I saw was the American Express office.' In the company of Kevin Norton, though she did not say so; and no sooner had her package been handed over the counter to her, than back they had rushed to their campsite far out in the countryside. No time, it had turned out, for the Coliseum, the Pantheon, or the Forum. Walt, it seemed, was eager to leave, even threatening to leave without them. 'In a way I think it was worse than if I hadn't gone at all.'

'But if you've been to Rome, and you're in Florence now, then you're backtracking. Heading home, are you?'

'No, it was an unexpected detour, something to do with an interview Kevin was supposed to do. After this, we head south.'

'And the campsites?' Ben asked, because she had suddenly looked so unhappy, and her frown had been like a cloud slipping over the sun. 'All terrible, were they?'

'No, not terrible,' Marianne said.

'Not all of them,' Gemma agreed. 'Some were, but come to think of it, some of them weren't too bad.'

'Ah,' Ben said, nodding. *And that*, he thought, *explains why it's been so hard to find you since Amsterdam.* He'd been searching in the cities, and they were at those campsites, where, it seemed, Gemma had been so unhappy. *And I was about to conclude that I'd have to contact Daddy and tell him it was a bust.*

'But you're in Italy,' he said aloud, 'and it'd be hard not to enjoy the scenery just about anywhere. This city, for instance, is one of the most beautiful cities in the world, people say often, and I have to say I agree.' He made an expansive gesture that took in the plaza about them. 'And before, if you came from Amsterdam, then you must've come through Germany, which can be very beautiful — and Austria . . . '

Both of them shook their heads.

'France,' Marianne said.

'And Switzerland,' Gemma added. 'And, yes, we've seen some beautiful scenery, especially in Switzerland. But after a while, even the Alps get boring. So when we realized we were camping only a few miles from Firenze, Florence, it seemed a crime not to try to see the city. So, like I said before, we've gone AWOL.'

He laughed. 'Okay, I can't say I blame you. If I was fifty miles away from Florence, or maybe even a hundred, I'd probably go AWOL too. So what's next on your journey, or is it back to Amsterdam?'

'No, we're going to Greece,' Gemma said. 'And from there, well, I'm not sure. It's sort of up to the driver. Istanbul, I think, and eventually India.' *But weren't we all supposed to have a voice in the itinerary?* she thought. *When did we agree to let Kevin and Walt make all the decisions for us? I don't remember that ever being discussed.*

'Greece. Now that's a coincidence,' Ben said. 'I was thinking of flying over to Athens myself. It's always been one of my favorite cities. Maybe we'll even be on the same flight. It'd be nice to travel with other Americans.'

'No, no airplanes. We'll be taking a ferry from someplace called Brindisi, down south. It's a vehicle ferry, so we'll drive right onto the boat, from what I understand, and right off again when we reach Greece. We couldn't do that on a plane.'

'No, I suppose you couldn't.'

'Plus the ferry's cheaper than flying,' Marianne said.

'I guess so. Well, if you want to contact me, you can always email here. You never know what might come up.' He found a scrap of paper in his pocket and wrote his email address on it, handing it to Gemma, who tucked it carefully into one pocket of her shirt. 'And when you get to Athens — '

'*If* we get to Athens,' Gemma cut him off.

'Which we probably won't,' Marianne said.

'Not unless there's a campsite close by,' Gemma added drily.

'I'm sure there's no shortage of campsites in Greece,' Ben said.

'But it has to be cheap,' Gemma said.

To which Ben could think of no suitable answer. He glanced across the plaza and saw a young man coming in their direction, all but running. His eyes, even at the distance, looked ablaze. *Kevin Norton*, Ben told himself, recognizing him at once from the photograph David Dolan had supplied him, the photograph he had studied and studied so that the likeness, just as the girls' likenesses, was branded on his memory.

Aloud, he said, 'Uh, those friends you mentioned — he wouldn't happen to be one of them, would he? Over there, coming to join us?'

They followed his glance. 'Oh,' Marianne said, and Gemma said, 'Damn! How did he find us so quickly?'

Ben laughed. 'Practically everyone who comes to Florence ends up in this piazza, at one of these cafés. It couldn't have been too hard for him to figure out. Hi,' he greeted an out-of-breath Kevin as he came up to the table. 'These pretty girls were sympathizing with me over a glass of wine. Would you like to join us?'

'Thanks, but I can't. The rest of our group is waiting to leave, as soon as I bring the runaway children home,' Kevin said, not even bothering to conceal his pique.

'We're not children,' Gemma said sharply. 'And we're not prisoners, either. No one told us the van was leaving this early. If they had, we would've been there and ready to go. But I thought we were leaving tomorrow, so we decided it was stupid to come all the way to Italy and not see a single one of these amazing cities.'

'But you did see Rome,' Kevin said.

'About as much of it as I might've seen from a speeding taxi. Anyway, here we were, close to Florence, so we caught a ride into town, and voila.'

'A ride?' His ears seemed to prick up at the mention. 'Caught a ride with who?'

'Not that it makes any difference to you,' Gemma replied, 'but if you have to know, with a nice couple from Peoria, who turned down our invitation to lunch

— a *real* lunch, not sandwiches from some podunk bar. And right now we were just about on our way to see the David — the real one in the Duomo, not the outdoor imitation — when Mr. Craig politely invited us to have a glass of wine with him. Which, I suppose, we won't be finishing, if according to you, everyone's waiting for us. Thank you.' She stood and offered Ben her hand. 'It's been really nice talking to you.'

'Yes,' Marianne said. 'We Americans . . . well, you know.'

Gemma swept grandly by Kevin Norton and started across the piazza, the other two trailing in her wake. They caught up with her halfway across.

'If you'd told me you had friends here,' Kevin said, 'we could have arranged for you to see them. You didn't have to sneak away.'

'He's not a friend. We just happened to run into him,' Gemma said. *But*, she thought, *I wish he was*. It had been very enjoyable to spend a few minutes with someone grown up for a change. Grown up, and rather attractive, but she did not think she should mention that.

'Ah,' was all he said, but then he thought of something, and added, 'And those sandwiches were cheap. That's why we had them instead of your so-called real lunch.'

* * *

Watching them go, Ben was struck again by how attractive Gemma Dolan was. Her father was probably wise to want to know who the girls were traveling with. At least now he had some progress to report.

And the information about Brindisi would be very helpful. He had contacts here in Italy, from his old days in intelligence. It had been a while, but intelligence operatives had long memories, and they were quick to do favors; you never knew when you would want one in return.

So it would not be difficult for him to learn which ferry they took, and where it landed. Wherever they were in Greece, now that he had picked up their trail, he would be able to stay close. Fortunately, he knew Greece well. And he had contacts there also, which would certainly prove useful.

David Dolan had told him he was not to think of extricating the girls unless it appeared there was some kind of trouble. But he feared that trouble had just appeared on the scene. Seeing Kevin Norton in person had jogged his memory in a way that his photograph had not.

Unless he was very much mistaken, he had at one time, back in his CIA days, read a file about that young man. Something to do with his activities in Berlin. Just at the present, the rest of the memory eluded him, but it would come back to him eventually. He was sure of it.

And whatever it was, he did not think it would be good news.

6

Ben Craig's friends in Italian intelligence were glad to hear what he had to tell them, especially about the garage in Amsterdam and the peculiar route the camper had taken from there to Florence.

'I think they might be visiting sleeper cells,' Ben said. 'But now that I've picked up the trail, I'll be able to determine that more accurately. And I promise I'll let you know anything I find out, though by then they'll probably have left Italy.'

'Nevertheless, anything we can learn will be useful, if not to us, then to our fellow intelligence agencies in other countries. And we will indeed keep a close watch on the traveling camper. If they take a ferry from Brindisi, be assured we will know of it — what boat, and where they land, which will almost certainly be Patras. It's where travelers to Greece nearly always disembark. It is only a relatively short drive from there to Athens.'

'Though a sometimes frightening drive,' one of the others said with a laugh.

'Frightening?' Ben asked.

'It's a mountain road. And some of the drivers like to travel it fast. So, yes, it can be a bit nerve-wracking for some of the passengers. But it's only an hour or so to Athens.'

Remembering what Gemma had told him back in Florence, Ben said, 'They might not be going to Athens.'

Which only earned him puzzled looks from the other men in the room.

'Well, of course, wherever they go, we will know,' he was assured. 'And we will let you know as well.'

★   ★   ★

But, as Ben had suspected, it was not at Patras that the group left the boat.

Gemma and Marianne were asleep in their cabin when the knock came at their door.

Marianne slept on, but Gemma, wakened by the rap at the door, stumbled across the darkened room.

'Who's there? she asked without opening the door.

'It's me. Time to get up,' Kevin said. 'We'll be disembarking soon. You've got enough time to grab yourselves a cup of coffee in the canteen, but you'll have to move it.'

'Disembarking?' Gemma blinked. 'But it's the middle of the night.' She looked at the porthole in the far wall and saw nothing beyond it but blackness. 'It's not even dawn yet. We can't possibly have reached Patras already.'

'No, not Patras. You're right about that,' he said. 'Come on, or you won't even have time for that coffee.'

And with that, he was gone. Gemma went back across the small cabin to rouse the still-sleeping Marianne.

As it turned out, they had to get the coffee to go; and even so, by the time they had reached the deck with their steaming cups, the ship's crew had already lowered the driving ramp down to the waiting dock. Walt was in line with the camper, third vehicle back from the front, and looking annoyed as the stragglers showed up.

'Where is this place?' Gemma asked, trying to rub the sleep from her eyes. The sky was just starting to lighten. Beyond the docks she could see distant mountains.

'Igoumenitsa,' Kevin informed her.

'*Gezundheit,*' she said. 'Ego-what?'

'Igoumenitsa,' he said again. 'The gateway to Macedonia.'

'And why,' she asked, 'are we traveling via the gateway to Macedonia, and not the gateway to Athens?' She hesitated for a moment. 'No, wait, let me guess. It's cheaper, right?'

Kevin snapped his fingers and grinned at her. 'You got it,' he said.

Gemma groaned. 'I should've stayed in bed.'

'We've got a long drive ahead of us,' he said. 'If you want to sleep for a while once we're on the road again, I'll wake you up in time.'

'In time for what?' she asked grumpily, 'To see the sights?'

'It's Macedonia,' he said drily, 'not the end of the earth.'

⋆　⋆　⋆

74

The camper with its motley crew of young people had scarcely driven down the boat's ramp before Ben got the news from his contacts of their somewhat unusual landing at the out-of-the-way port of Igoumenitsa. Which, he realized, soon following close on their trail, gave him one advantage, at least: it would indeed be much easier to track them across the wilds of Macedonia than it might have been trying to follow them in the bustling city of Athens, even with the help of his old friend Miko Stavros in Greek intelligence.

But while that was to his advantage, what on earth kind of advantage, he wondered, could it possibly offer a busload of young people trying to see the world? Unless their goal was to see beaches deserted in the fishing off-season, as the one below him now certainly was. And other than the fishermen who came here in season, no one was likely to be seeking this particular seaside. It was simply too far off the beaten track to appeal even to those travelers who might be considered antisocial extremists.

He looked down once at his feet to check his footing. He was at the moment standing on a rocky and somewhat perilous outcrop above the spot where they had chosen to camp, and the last thing he wanted to do was take a fall because some rock had shifted under his foot.

He changed his stance slightly, testing the rock upon which he was standing to be sure it was solid, and lifted his binoculars once again to his eyes, moving them back and forth in yet another attempt to find either Marianne Marker or Gemma Dolan. So far, he had seen nothing of either of them.

Just then, Gemma walked into view on the sand below. Walking beside her was Kevin Norton. It was too far to hear what they were saying, but at a glance it looked as if they were quarreling. Certainly Gemma looked none too pleased with things as she too surveyed the barren beach.

★　★　★

'I thought you said this wasn't the end of the earth,' Gemma told Kevin unhappily. 'But if you asked me, I'd say this looks to me *exactly* like the end of the earth. I thought I'd seen some desolate places on this trip, but this is the worst one yet. It's not even a real campsite. What are we supposed to do about toilets, or showers, or even food? There's nothing here. Absolutely nothing.'

Kevin followed her glance. Even he had to admit, at least privately, that the place was pretty forlorn: not even a regulated campsite, it was nothing more than a long, desolate strip of beach with a few puny shrubs here and there and one dreary tree, and in the distance a row of fishermen's huts, empty now. The wind blowing in from the bay had a definite chill to it, and the sky was a pewter gray. Only a distant taverna, its lights faintly aglow, offered any relief from the bleak aspect before them, and it seemed to offer asylum rather than cheer.

Still, that was hardly an opinion he could offer his companion. His job was to quell any rebellion on the part of their fellow travelers, not foster it.

'I wouldn't exactly say there's nothing, here, Gemma. You can bathe in the ocean, you know,' he said. 'And, after all, sand is sand, isn't it? What I mean is, it's a beach, and we can work on our suntans here just as well as at one of the popular beaches. And those are crowded at this time of year.'

'But the tourist season must be over by now,' Gemma said.

'It is,' he agreed. 'For most of Europe. But this is Greece. People come here in the off-season from all over Europe, from the Scandinavian countries especially, for the sun and the beaches. Which just means that the good beaches in Greece, the resort beaches, stay popular all year. Too popular and too rich for our blood, sorry to say. Walt even called ahead to check on reservations, and this was one of the few places where they could still accommodate us and that wouldn't have cost us an arm and a leg.'

'A price I think I'd be willing to pay,' Gemma said, 'if anyone had asked me. Which, as usual, no one did. Don't the rest of us have any say at all in your plans?'

He laughed at that suggestion. 'Come on, Gemma, don't be a spoilsport. And as for the rest of your complaints, there's that taverna in the distance. Close enough that we can walk to it.' And where he was to meet his next contacts, two men from a local terrorist cell, but of course he could not tell her that. 'I'm sure they'll let us use their toilet facilities,' he said instead. 'And they're bound to have food.'

'It's easy for you to laugh,' she said, turning on him. 'You've managed to get into every city that the rest of us have missed out on. You and Walt.'

'That's not fair,' he said. 'I had money to pick up along the way.'

'Which I expected to be able to do, too.'

'That's different. Your father will be sending you a fat allowance check each month, in one big lump. I told you at the start, my uncle Ralph would be sending mine in dribs and drabs. I suppose it's his way of cutting back on my spending. If I don't have it, I can't squander it. You can understand that, can't you?'

She nodded begrudgingly. He always made her feel guilty somehow because she was a little better off than the others. It wasn't as if her father and stepmother were genuinely rich, either. They were, as she had tried often to make him understand, no more than upper middle class. At which he had always laughed.

'Upper middle class to you means rich to pretty much everyone else,' he usually replied. 'And besides,' he added, 'I'm trying to work in some journalistic pieces as we go — that's the career I want. Which means I have to go where the interviews are. So yes, it means I have to make trips into the cities. But we've picked the campsites that'd be the least expensive for everyone, and still have reasonable accommodation.'

Gemma waved a hand to indicate the forlorn beach before them. 'This is your idea of reasonable accommodation?' she asked in a voice dripping with scorn. 'I don't see anything reasonable about it.'

'It doesn't look that bad to me,' he said. 'Like I said, it's a beach, and we have the same sun they have at the swankier places.'

'Which right now is none, or hardly any,' she said, glancing skyward.

'It'll show up. This is Greece. And as for Walt, the camper's his responsibility, and that includes keeping it running. He's had to pick up parts as we go. That's why he's had to travel into the cities. They don't stock a lot of parts in remote places. Where would he get parts for the camper here, for example? Do you think they might stock them at that taverna over there?'

'I'm sure they don't,' she conceded. 'But he's needed a lot of parts, in that case.'

'The van's not exactly new. Maybe you're used to traveling by limousine, but for the rest of us . . . '

'I am not,' she retorted. 'Which you know full well. In Paris I walked, or I took the Metro. You always make me sound like some pampered princess. It's not fair.'

'As a matter of fact,' he added, ignoring her outcry, 'speaking of the van, I think Walt has plans to take it into a shop while we're here, for a major check-up. Probably a three- or four-day job, he said. And I suppose that means he'll have it done in Athens.'

'In Athens? While we cool our heels here at the end of the earth, right? And what about you? I suppose you have another one of your uncle's checks to pick up. In Athens, too, huh?'

'No,' he said, speaking slowly, 'not a check from my uncle. But I did have a letter back in Rome from some old friends who are living in Athens now. They asked me to come see them if I was anywhere close, and I wrote back to tell them I would. I think it'd be rude of me not to, since I told them I'd see them when I got here.'

'So you two get to go to Athens, and the rest of us will be left here twiddling our thumbs. And, how did you put it? Oh, yes, working on our suntans?'

'Look, I'll tell you what we'll do,' he said in his most conciliatory tone. 'I think Walt was planning on driving north to Turkey. Not Istanbul, exactly; I think the idea was to stop in Bursa.'

'Not Istanbul? No Topkapi, no Blue Mosque . . . ?' Gemma was practically sputtering. 'We can't miss all of that. Not like Rome. Not again.'

'But you'll like Bursa, I promise,' he said. 'It was the capitol once, and I've heard it's worth a visit. And from there, well, how about if I talk to Walt and see if I can convince him to drive straight across to India? How does Delhi sound? Big city-ish enough for you?'

'I've always wanted to see Delhi,' she admitted, softening a bit. Still, to be in Turkey and not see Istanbul . . . ? Surely that was the very definition of folly. As bad as driving through Italy and not seeing Rome. Or Florence, which they would not have seen either if she had not taken matters into her own hands.

'Then that's it,' he said, relieved. 'Delhi it is. I'll find some way to convince Walt. And I'm sorry if you don't think I've been fair. Now, in the meantime, I'm hungry, and I've heard good things about the food in that taverna too. How about we go there and get a bite to eat?'

'Heard good things where?' she asked,

her face scrunched up in suspicion.

He realized his mistake too late. 'Actually, Walt has a guidebook, which I'm not supposed to mention. And if you're wondering why you've never seen it, it's because he treats it mostly like it's top secret.'

'Why?' she asked.

'If you're asking me why no one else gets to look at it but him, the answer is I don't know. It's just the way Walt is. He likes to feel like he's running the show, I guess. But he did tell me he checked and found that tavern listed in it, with a three-star rating. That's pretty amazing, for a place so out of the way.'

'Out of the way is right.' She thought for a moment. 'Last night, when we turned off the main highway,' (which was only a few meters away, but she did not point that out) 'didn't I see a motel? A nice modern one. Which I'm sure would have a dining room . . . '

'Reserved for the tourists on the tour buses,' he said quickly. 'You did see the tour buses, didn't you?' (She hadn't, and her expression must have told him so) 'No?

84

Well, those motels are all government-operated here. That's how they do things in Greece. And the dining room is only for people who've pre-booked and pre-paid. And who've arrived on those buses, all neatly set up beforehand. But the point is, we're in Greece, and this isn't a spur-of-the-moment kind of society.'

'But if that true, then that taverna . . . '

' . . . Is almost certainly not a government operation,' he finished for her. 'Probably it's being run by some struggling widow trying to care for her family with whatever meager income she can earn from the place. You wouldn't want to deprive the poor woman of the few drachmas our meals would give to her, would you?'

'I suppose not,' she replied sulkily.

They were interrupted as their travel companions, without Walt, climbed out of the camper just then. Marianne was first, followed by Denise, the petite French girl who had signed on with them back in Paris; and behind them, the two other men: Anders the Swede and Marco the Italian.

'Walt is tinkering with the air conditioning,' Anders said. 'He says there was something wrong with it on the drive across Greece.'

'It seemed fine to me,' Gemma said.

'We've decided,' Marco, the ever-diligent guide, said, sweeping his hand from side to side to indicate the dark rolling water before them, 'that this is the Thermaic Gulf.'

'And in this direction,' Anders said, pointing more or less northward, 'is Salonika. Or, if you prefer the old Greek name, Thessalonica.'

'And Athens?' Marianne asked hopefully. 'Which way is that?'

'That way.' Marco pointed. 'But, alas, a very long distance that way.'

'Too far to walk,' Gemma said. 'And apparently not on our intended route.'

'We were about to visit that taverna over there,' Kevin said, pointing in its direction and effectively cutting off that line of conversation, 'and seeing about getting a bite to eat. Anyone want to join us?'

'What about Walt?' Marianne asked.

'He's tinkering,' Anders said.

'With the perfectly fine air conditioner,' Gemma said.

'Come on, let's go,' Marco said. 'Walt's a big boy. He can catch up with us later, or not. Now that you mention it, I am sort of hungry.'

The others voiced their agreement, and, noisy and laughing, they started in a gaggle across the sand. Kevin raised an eyebrow in Gemma's direction.

'Well, we do have to eat. Something,' she said. She started after the group, and Kevin hurried to catch up with her.

7

Notwithstanding that she was feeling crabby, Gemma had to admit that the taverna was better than it had looked at a distance. It was bare and unpretentious, and the wood outside had been scoured and bleached by ocean and sand. But inside it was clean at least, and the proprietress and pair of youngsters who Gemma thought were perhaps a nephew and niece went out of their way to make the visitors feel welcome.

She tried only one bite of the octopus — pickled, Kevin told her; but pickled or not, it still looking unappetizingly raw to her, though the boys ate it bravely enough, pronouncing with each bite (and over-enthusiastically, she thought) how delicious it was; and the resinated wine tasted, as to her mind it always did, like turpentine.

But the black bread was tasty and still warm from its time in the oven, and there was plenty of fresh butter to be slathered on the thick slabs; and the fish (bream, perhaps?) charred and served adorned with nothing more than some slices of lemon, could not have been more than an hour or so out of the sea.

Nor, she thought, could it have been more delicious.

*　*　*

When the knock sounded on the door of the camper, Walt carefully slid the concealing shelves back over the radio equipment hidden in the side of the van where, so far at least, none of the customs officials had even suspected its presence. You might have supposed, he had thought every time they had gone through an inspection, that someone would notice the discrepancy in the width of the camper's wall at that point, but so far no one had.

'Yes?' he called, and when Kevin called from outside, 'It's me,' Walt called back, 'Don't you have your key?'

'I do,' Kevin said, letting himself in. 'I

just wanted to warn you.'

'Thanks. I appreciate that. I trust you are alone,' he said, looking over Kevin's shoulder. 'Where is everyone else?'

'I left them contentedly finishing their dinner at the taverna. Your absence was noticed, by the way.'

'It couldn't be helped, I'm afraid. I had reports to make,' Walt said; and then, thinking he might have been too brusque, he said, 'No one was terribly upset, I hope.'

'Gemma . . . '

'I've always said she was the most dangerous one,' Walt said. 'What did she have to grumble about this time?'

'She was not exactly smitten with this location.'

'Too bad. This was where we were instructed to go. You know that.'

'I do. Don't worry about Gemma, she'll get over it,' Kevin said sharply. 'Besides, I can handle her.'

'Like you handled her in Florence?' Walt asked.

'That was nothing. A harmless tantrum from two spoiled American brats is all.

They just wanted to have a decent lunch. And that was where I found them, as a matter of fact, at one of the cafés, just finishing their lunch. So it was exactly what they said it was, and there was no harm done.'

'But there might have been.'

'Yes, I will concede that. There might have been.'

'And we would have to report that to Ralph.'

'Perhaps.'

'No perhaps about it. My instructions are to report anything to him that is even slightly out of the ordinary. Are you disputing that?'

'Not at all. Don't be so quick to take offense.'

'Well, then . . . you do realize I reported that stranger to Ralph — the one they met there?'

'Why?'

'Why? For the reason I just explained. My instructions are to report anything out of the ordinary.'

'There was no reason for alarm. He was just a stranger, a passing American.

It's an odd American habit they have, to consider every other American they meet in a foreign country as if they were long-lost friends. It is of no consequence.'

'If you say so,' Walt said. He had not told Kevin that his instructions had been to use his judgment in dealing with Gemma Dolan. 'She will be useful in time,' Ralph had said, 'But not if she jeopardizes your other assignments, which are paramount.'

So Walt had done what he thought best in that regard, but he thought it wisest if he did not share that information with Kevin. Instead, he said, 'I have my own ideas about how to quell any complaints. Look what I picked up in Turkey.'

He took a small box from his pocket and opened it. Inside, resting on a slip of cotton, was a syringe and a vial.

'What is it?' Kevin asked.

'So far as they will be concerned, I will be giving them shots as protection against malaria. It will keep them plenty docile, though.'

Kevin frowned. 'If we were caught smuggling drugs . . . '

'We have been through, what, five, six customs checkpoints, and no one has even suspected there was anything amiss.'

'A good thing, too,' Kevin said. 'We'd have a hard time explaining even your radio equipment. But drugs? Is that wise?'

'By the time we go through another checkpoint, everything will be labeled and looking perfectly innocent. Unless some-one were to do a chemical analysis, which is highly unlikely at a border checkpoint, no one will suspect anything. And I tell you, it will stop a lot of the questions people have been asking. People like Gemma Dolan. She must be kept in line. She cannot be allowed to interfere in our contacts along the way.'

'She won't. I mean to see to that.'

'So long as you have not fallen in love with her,' Walt added, watching him closely for any reaction.

'Me? In love?' Kevin looked properly amused at the suggestion. 'I've never been in love with anyone. Though I will admit to a sneaking affection for myself.'

They both laughed at that, but while Kevin was laughing, he found himself wondering: what if Walt was right? He had never met anyone like Gemma. She was the first woman he had ever known who was apparently immune to his charms, his every blandishment. By now, she should have been his slave. She should have been in love with him. He had started out fervently wishing that she might fall in love with him, and soon.

But it was beginning to look as if it had happened the other way round.

★   ★   ★

Gemma had lingered behind for a final cup of coffee when the others finished and started back to the camper. So she was alone when she left the taverna.

She was halfway across the lonely expanse of beach when she heard a sound behind her and looked back, to see two men rushing toward her. One of them held a knife, glinting in the pale moonlight.

She screamed and tried to run, but the unaccustomed sand made for slow going. She lost her balance and fell. Within seconds, they were upon her. The man with the knife raised it as if to stab her with it, when a nearby voice, a voice she knew, cried, 'What's going on here?'

'Kevin,' she screamed, 'help!'

'I'm coming,' he shouted back.

Her attackers looked in his direction, and then as suddenly as they had appeared, they were gone. She struggled to sit up in the sand, and saw them running away. In a moment, they had vanished into the darkness, and Kevin was kneeling beside her.

'Are you all right?' he asked, helping her up and enfolding her in an embrace. 'What happened?'

'Two men, they attacked me. They went that way,' she said, pointing; but when Kevin would have gone after them, she grabbed hold of his sleeve. 'No, don't,' she said. 'They're gone now. I think they wanted to rob me. An American woman, alone. I probably looked like easy prey, but you scared them off.'

'Thank god I came along when I did,' he said.

'Yes, thank god,' she echoed his words.

'But why were you coming this way in the first place?'

'I was looking for you,' he said. 'When the others got back to the camper and you weren't with them, I started worrying. I'd just left when I saw the kerfuffle, and I heard you scream. You're sure you're all right?'

'Yes, I am now. Thanks to you.'

For a moment more, Kevin continued to stare after the two who had attacked her. He was pretty sure he had recognized them, even in the dim light. Members of the local cell.

But everyone knew Gemma was with them. No one would have dared to attack her without orders from someone above them; and the only one who could have given those orders, apart from himself, was Walt.

But Walt would not have taken that kind of initiative, not without having received his own orders. Which meant, if not in so many words, Ralph must have said something that encouraged Walt to take the action he had.

Ben Craig. Walt had reported the

stranger the girls had met in Florence, and not long after, Gemma was attacked by, he was sure of it, two men from the local cell. It could be mere coincidence. Or maybe not.

'Look,' he said aloud, 'there wasn't any real harm done, right?'

'I guess not. I'm just a little shaken. Why? What are you thinking?'

'I'm thinking it might be best if we kept this to ourselves. If we reported it to the local police . . . well, I know what things are like in this part of the world. We'd be stuck here forever while they conducted an investigation, which probably wouldn't find anything. It'd all turn out to be a big waste of time. You don't really want to spend a couple of weeks here, do you?'

'No,' she agreed reluctantly. 'But shouldn't the others at least know what happened?'

'Nothing really did happen, did it?'

'No, I guess it didn't. But . . . '

'But from now on, I'll keep a closer watch on you,' he said.

'But Marianne. And Denise . . . '

'On them, too,' he said.

8

Unable to have a proper bath, Gemma had settled for a quick dip in the cold waters of the bay, all the while keeping an eye on the beach. There was something to be said for a beach as desolate as this one. The moon had risen by this time, and in its silvery glow she could see anyone approaching ages before they got to her. But, in fact, she had little expectation of seeing her attackers again. They had taken advantage of an opportunity that presented itself. They thought she looked like easy prey, and they had been scared off by Kevin's arrival. It was highly unlikely they had stayed in the neighborhood to try again.

By the time she had dried herself off using her clothing, and finally climbed into her berth in the camper, the others were already asleep, the girls in the berths by hers, the men in their sleeping bags outside on the beach. And they were all out like a light, she thought. Were they just all exhausted? Or was it the malaria shots Kevin had mentioned?

'Marianne,' she whispered, giving her friends' shoulder a gentle shake; but Marianne was apparently dead to the world. She only grunted and rolled over on her other side.

'Wish I could sleep that soundly,' Gemma said to herself.

But she did not. She woke early from a fitful sleep, and deciding she was hungry for some breakfast, she wriggled her way out of the cramped berth and went outside, planning to ask Kevin if he wanted to join her.

Kevin, however, was not in his sleeping bag, which was always the one just outside the camper's door. (As if he were guarding it? she had wondered more than once. Guarding the door, or guarding her?) She looked across the sand at the distant taverna, its lights on despite the early hour. Or maybe they just stayed on all night? It seemed extravagant for someone struggling, as Kevin had led her to believe the proprietress was.

But perhaps they had just been turned on a few minutes earlier. She had not noticed them when she went in the night before. Kevin had promised to keep an eye on her, but it was morning now, the sun just peeking over the horizon, and surely she was safe from would-be robbers in the daylight. Perhaps knowing this, Kevin had already gone looking for breakfast himself. She trudged dutifully in the direction of the distant lights, half convinced she would find him there, already eating.

Kevin was not inside the taverna, however, when she got there. A pair of fishermen were the only customers at this hour. They were sharing one of the small tables and apparently making a kind of breakfast of the leftover octopus from the night before. Gemma shuddered at that prospect, and assuring the madame that she was only looking for someone, she went back outside.

Once outside, however, she again thought of that motel off the main highway. Not too far distant for an early hike, especially in the cool morning air.

And she felt confident that she was in no danger of again being assaulted, not in daylight.

She was more mindful of Kevin's warning: that the dining room only served those who arrived on the tourist buses. But surely if she pleaded earnestly enough, and if she had enough money in hand (luckily she had spent almost nothing of her last allowance; where would she have spent it, anyway?) someone would take pity on her and scramble up some eggs at least, or whatever they did here for breakfast, so long as it involved no octopus.

The motel was indeed within walking distance. It took her no more than twenty minutes, and she noted as she crossed the parking lot that there were no tourist buses to be seen, only a solitary car; a rental from the looks of it. So much for that concern.

The lobby was deserted. She had anticipated someone standing guard inside the glass doors, refusing her entrance. Across the empty room, a sign above a door identified the room beyond in Greek she could not read, and in French *salle de manger*, which meant 'dining room'. She went to that and paused in the doorway.

The dining room too was empty, or nearly so. Only one table was occupied, and when she saw who was seated at the table sipping a cup of coffee, she gasped in astonishment.

'Mr. Craig,' she exclaimed, hurrying toward his table, 'am I glad to see you again.'

'Gemma?' He stood up, as surprised as she, and they embraced briefly.

'But what on earth brings you to this godforsaken corner of the world?' she asked.

'I was about to ask you the same thing,' he said, neatly sidestepping the necessity of an answer. 'Please,' he said, gesturing to the empty chair across from his, 'will you have some breakfast?'

'Oh, you wonderful man,' she sighed, sinking into the offered chair. 'But I thought they only served the prepaid tourists. The ones who came on the buses.'

He looked around the dining room. 'Oh, I think these folks are thankful for any business they can get. But what will you have?' He waved a hand, and a young man appeared from what she supposed was the kitchen, hurrying to the table.

'Anything, as long as it isn't octopus.'

He laughed. 'They do okay with eggs here, if you don't mind having them scrambled. No bacon, but I'm sure we can find you a lamp chop or two. The Greeks always have some lamb.'

'Just the eggs, and scrambled will be fine. And some coffee, please. Real coffee. I didn't know there was so much instant coffee in the world. Even worse, they make it with tepid water. At least they do at that taverna on the beach.'

'Hot water's a bit of a luxury in this corner of the world. But they make good real coffee here, and I promise you it's hot.' He gave the waiter the order in what sounded to her like more than competent Greek. 'Now,' he said to her when the waiter had returned to the kitchen, 'how's your trip around the world going?'

'It isn't, obviously, or I wouldn't be here. But what about you? This is an odd place to bump into you.'

'Not that odd. I'm on my way to Athens, but the drive was a little long to make in one day, so I stopped here for the night.' Which completely avoided the issue of what he was doing on this particular route anyway. He could hardly explain that he was here only because she was nearby.

'Athens?' Her eyes got a dreamy look in them.

'From here, it's a straight run down that highway out there.'

'And you're traveling alone?' Her look went from dreamy to mischievous.

He spread his hands to indicate the otherwise empty table.

'How would you feel,' she went on quickly, 'about a couple of hitchhikers?'

'You, you mean? And your friend — what was her name, Marianne?'

'Yes. Marianne. And, yes, me.'

'Sure,' he told her. 'But does this mean you're planning to go AWOL again?'

'I am. Maybe even permanently this time. But I have to go get Marianne. She's back in the camper, still asleep, as far as I know. Can you give me half an hour? Or maybe a bit more than that? I'll run, I promise.'

'No need to run. Take all the time you need. I've still got to pack, settle my bill, all that business. And I think I saw some gas pumps outside, so I'll fill up the car while I'm here. If I'm not still at the pumps when you get back, I'll wait for you in the parking lot. It's the gray Fiat.'

'I'll find you,' she said. Her scrambled eggs and coffee had arrived. She wolfed them down, thinking now of far more important things than breakfast, and got hastily up from her chair 'Don't leave without us, please.'

'I wouldn't dream of it,' he said, and meant it.

He was thinking he would have to resend his last report to David Dolan.

9

They had only a few days in Athens, but Gemma had to admit it was the most she had enjoyed herself since they had left Paris. Excepting, she amended, that brief visit to Florence. Nor could she entirely dismiss the fact that Ben Craig had figured in both outings.

'I think he's got a crush on you,' Marianne had said when Gemma, with exaggerated nonchalance, had mentioned this to her.

'He probably just thinks he's helping a pair of errant waifs,' Gemma replied. 'But he's nice, isn't he?'

'I think he's to die for.'

'Well, yes,' Gemma agreed. 'He's kind of sexy, I guess. But you have a thing for older men.'

'He's not that much older than us. He's thirty-two, as a matter of fact. Don't look at me like that — I only know that because I asked him. Not straight up, but kind of sideways, if you know what I mean. And you're twenty-one. That's not like the end of the world. Not a May-December kind of thing.'

Gemma . . . ' Marianne started, and hesitated, looking about dazedly as if she had forgotten where they were, or why. Finally she pulled her shoulders back and made a noticeable effort to get herself together.

'What you said the other day,' she said, 'about maybe not going back? To the van, to the trip, I mean. You weren't serious, were you?'

'I was. I am,' Gemma said. 'I haven't been having any fun; not the way I thought I'd be, anyway. And you can't tell me that you aren't getting tired of it too. Washing your clothes every day and hanging them wherever you can find to dry, and never getting a bath where you can soak for hours without someone tapping on the door to remind you that they're waiting. Not to mention the cramped accommodation.'

'But we knew it'd be cramped before we even started out,' Marianne said,

107

seizing upon the one thing she knew she could defend. 'Besides, I gave Walt Prescott practically every penny I had to my name, right up front. I only have enough money left in the bank to buy the cheapest ticket back to Dayton, and that's probably only if I offer to serve cocktails to the other passengers. It's different for you, I realize that, but I can't afford to walk away from the trip at this point. Besides, didn't you leave Kevin a note when we left the beach, promising him that we'd be back?'

'I left him a note saying we'd catch up with them in Istanbul.' And telling him she and Marianne were going into Athens, where he had not the slightest chance of finding them without any more information than that. She had even avoided the main square just in case he was looking for them there. A warning Ben had given her in Florence, and which she had taken to heart.

But a nagging thought kept running through her mind. Where had Kevin been when they left to travel to Athens with Ben Craig? Hadn't he, just the night before, promised to keep a close eye on her? And, yes, he could assume, as she had, that she was safe in the light of day. But still, to just disappear without a word ... and where had he gone, anyway? Supposedly there were no cities near.

'Well, don't you feel any obligation to keep your word?' Marianne asked.

'To meet up with them there? But that's in four days' time. At least, if they stick to the schedule. That was when they planned to be in Istanbul, in any case; but who knows what they really will do or when they'll actually show up?'

That at least, though she did not say this, was when Kevin and Walt had planned to be in Istanbul. She seriously doubted that the rest of them would see anything of the city. Where was it Kevin had mentioned to her that they were staying instead? Bursa? That barely got a mention in the guidebook she had purchased in Athens.

'I did some asking around,' Marianne went on, speaking quickly now, 'and there's a freighter leaving from Piraeus; that's the port for Athens. It leaves early tomorrow morning for Istanbul, with only one stop along the way, at Lesbos. It'll get us to Istanbul in plenty of time, and even with an extra day for sightseeing in the city. You'd like that, wouldn't you? You've said so much about all the things you wanted to see in Istanbul.' She paused for a breath, and added on a plaintive note, 'Plus it's cheap. Meaning I can afford it.'

'And you've already looked into this?' Gemma laughed. 'You must've had the idea for a while now.'

'Don't be mad at me, please. If we take that freighter, we can have a day or so in Istanbul and still be back with the group in plenty of time, no harm done.'

'You can't believe Kevin won't be angry.'

'Totally pissed off, I bet. Same as he was in Florence. But he'll get over it,' Marianne said. *Because he's in love with you, damn it*, she thought but did not say. Why was it every man she found herself attracted to ended up in love with her best friend? Ben Craig, for instance. What would she not give to have him look at her the way he looked at Gemma when he thought she was not watching?

Not that she could blame any of them. She was in love with Gemma too, in her own way. But it was frustrating, nevertheless, always to be the third wheel on the bicycle.

'I guess,' Gemma conceded, 'if you've got your heart set on it.'

'I don't, but I think it's the best thing to do.'

10

'Are you sure?' Ben asked when they told him they had booked passage on the freighter. 'We could fly back to Paris from Athens. Or to Washington, even. I'll pay for the tickets, if that's a problem.'

'Of course we couldn't let you do that,' Gemma had said. 'No, this is best. As a matter of fact, both of us have already paid for our trip in the camper. Anyway, I should have money waiting for me in Istanbul. I have no idea how to try to get it back if I don't claim it on time.'

Of course, he could not very well explain that the tickets would not be on him at all, but on her father. Nor that their trip to Istanbul was going to make things very much more difficult for him. He could not very well just show up once again out of the blue without blowing his cover. As it was, he was grateful that Gemma, in her surprise and delight at getting to spend time in Athens, had forgotten how unlikely it was that he should have been in the far northern reaches of Greece at the same time as her.

Nor could he tell her without explaining everything that he had finally remembered that file on Kevin Norton, who had at one time gone by the name of Kurt Reidl, and that under that name there was a warrant out for his arrest back in Hamburg for suspicion of murdering a young Jewish woman by the name of Bridget Klein.

Plus, his time in northern Greece had given him the opportunity to investigate just what Kevin Norton was doing on this trip. Information that he intended to share with intelligence agencies along the way, in the various countries that he and the camper visited.

Even if he told her everything — and he could hardly explain about Norton without telling her who he was and how he happened to be following her and her friends across Europe — he was not at all sure how she would react. She was sure to be angry with him. Angry enough that she might very well refuse to do what he wanted her to do, what her father surely would insist upon, which was to return to Washington with him.

So there was nothing he could do but see them off the following morning after arranging for someone to keep an eye on them for at least part of the trip. Someone from his previous line of work, although Alexei Dragoumis was retired now.

'I'll only be going as far as Lesbos,' Alexei told him. 'That's where I live these days. But I have a friend who is part of the ship's crew. I'll give him a small stipend to keep an eye on them for the second leg of the journey.' He gave Ben a meaningful look.

'Of course,' Ben said quickly, and counted out a number of bills from his wallet. 'Just see that they arrive in Istanbul unmolested.'

'You can count on me,' Alexei assured him, 'and my friend.' He pocketed the money with a satisfied smile. It was rather more, he was thinking, than he had anticipated. His friend would be pleased with even a fraction of that.

Before he saw the girls aboard the

freighter, however, Ben made sure that his Turkish 'friends' would be on the lookout for them at their end. And he made sure once again that Gemma knew how to get in touch with him if the need arose; not just his email this time, but his cellphone number as well.

'Wherever you are,' he assured her. 'If you call, I'll come. Right away. I promise.'

'That's very gallant,' she said with a grateful smile. 'And potentially very expensive.'

'Don't think about that for a minute. I mean it — I'll be there as soon as I can.' And, of course, he did not intend to be very far away if that should happen.

But he could not tell her that either.

11

Which was how they had left it.

But now, standing by the railing on the deck of that freighter, with the night fading slowly into dawn, Gemma found herself thinking of the morning when her path had crossed Ben's at that motel in northern Greece, and wondering once again what on earth Ben Craig had been doing there. Yes, he had said he was driving to Athens, but from where? Unless he had been coming down from Albania, which seemed most unlikely, there was no reason for anyone even to have been there.

Which, of course, could have been said as well of their little band. Why on earth had they been there? She had seen Kevin one very late evening talking outside the taverna with the two fishermen they had seen there; a meeting he had never mentioned to her. Indeed, the next time they had seen the same two, and she was sure they were the same, though all three men had pretended they did not know one another.

So obviously Kevin had some reason for going there, some reason he was not sharing with her. But what could be the purpose of it?

And on the drive to Athens with Ben, they had passed other campsites. None of them had looked as if they were filled to capacity, which was the excuse she, they, had been given for staying where they had. She had looked specifically.

Of course, it was true that she had no idea how expensive any of these places might be. Kevin had emphasized the money factor, and that might well be the real reason, but it did almost seem as if Kevin and Walt were purposefully avoiding major cities.

She thought of the places they had stayed instead. All of them had been out of the way, sometimes outrageously so. Had Kevin had other meetings along the way, meetings of which the rest of them remained ignorant?

But, no, not all of them were ignorant,

surely. Wherever Kevin had gone, it was only with the connivance of Walt. He was the one driving, the one who owned the camper. And the one making most of the major decisions for them, it would seem, although Kevin did appear to have some sort of an 'in' with him. Perhaps it was only that they were old friends.

Which only reminded her once again of their initial meeting, not at the opera, but at lunch the following day. She was sure Kevin had said then, or had at least implied, that he knew no one in Paris; but almost immediately afterward he had said he was there to visit his old friend, Walt. Or had Marianne been the one to imply his loneliness? She was not sure now.

Whatever their relationship, however, it was still clear that their itinerary was mostly Walt's choice. So the blame was mostly on Walt, though Kevin couldn't escape some of it as well.

But, blame for what? For trying to save everyone some money, which was more often than not the excuse they had given? And everyone had been grateful for that, even Gemma, who knew perfectly well

118

she was better off in that respect than the others were. But she still could not understand it.

The sun was rising now, accompanied by a slight breeze. The sea, like glass only a short while earlier, now had little caps of white on the waves. In the distance she could just make out what she thought was the skyline of Istanbul.

She looked over her shoulder. Marianne was still sleeping restlessly on the freighter's deck, using her duffel bag for a pillow. Gemma decided she would let her sleep for a few minutes more. At the rate this old tub traveled, that skyline which looked so close could still be hours away.

It had been, by any standard, a hellish trip. At least for the first leg, from Athens to the isle of Lesbos, they'd had the company of that delightful Greek man, the better-than-plump Mister Dragoumis, who had more or less taken them under his wing.

'Avoid the food as much as you can,' he had advised them from the beginning. 'There's usually melon on the buffet, or some kind of fruit. Eat that for these next two days. And the coffee is excellent if you get hold of it before they put the sugar in it, which will rot your teeth right out of your pretty heads. And don't let them even dream you have American dollars. In fact, keep your hands tight on your drachmas as well. The captain is all right — I've sailed with him before — but most of his crew aren't much more than modern-day pirates. And we'll sleep on the deck; never mind those filthy cabins they've assigned us. The nights are warm here and it'll be safer that way. Plus, you won't go home with any hitchhikers. Bugs,' he added when they gave him puzzled looks.

He had been right about the cabins, too, though both girls had needed to see for themselves the dirty blankets and thin straw mattresses that were so insect-infested that they seemed to be in some sort of perpetual motion before they decided he was right and settled for sleeping on the deck. There he provided a massive and well-padded barricade between them and any overeager crew members, many of whom did indeed look like extras out of a pirate movie. Gemma kept waiting for Long John Silver himself to make an appearance.

But the amiable Mister Dragoumis had left the ship at Lesbos, leaving them to do the final leg, another night, on their own. And Gemma had spent most of that night awake, just to be safe. There had been one crew member in particular, a huge burly fellow who had seemed to have attached himself to them. He was rarely far out of sight, and since he seemed to have an eye on them, Gemma had made a point of keep an eye on him as well.

Now, with the dawn and Istanbul approaching, she had gotten up and gone to the rail to watch for the arrival of both. To do so, she had actually to step over the sleeping crewman only a few feet from where they had bedded down on the deck. She had not even been aware that he was sleeping topside with them, and so close.

Well, she told herself with grim satisfaction, his vigil and hers would soon be ended.

12

They had reached Istanbul at last.

Or, they were at least in the home stretch; but something seemed not quite right in customs. The two men at the table before Gemma apparently spoke no English beyond, 'You speak Turkish?' which they had asked when the girls first walked up to their table. After which they kept looking back and forth, from the girls to their passports to their measly duffel bags, and back to the girls again.

Surely, Gemma thought, *they can't suspect we're trying to smuggle anything*. But, wait, hadn't she seen a movie some years back about an American trying to smuggle drugs — was it pot? — out of Turkey? *The Midnight Express*, if she remembered the movie's title right.

And it was supposed to have been based on real events. So maybe all young Americans were automatically suspect to these inspectors. But how did you reassure these grim-looking men on that subject without actually making them more suspicious? If she said to them, bluntly, 'Look, we don't have any drugs on us — I don't even smoke regular cigarettes, neither of us do,' they would almost certainly assume the opposite.

She had noticed while they waited that both of them kept glancing behind at a closed door; so when it finally opened, she supposed they had been waiting for the man who entered through it.

'Colonel,' one of them greeted him; and although the two at the table remained seated, one had the impression that both of them had just snapped to attention.

The newcomer was tall and lean, with the same piercing dark eyes that the other two agents had. Eyes that, as he crossed the room toward them, regarded her and Marianne closely, looking them both up and down in what could only be described as a suspicious manner.

When he had reached the table before which they were standing, he said in perfectly good if accented English, 'You are American, yes?'

'Yes, we are,' Gemma said; and Marianne, who seemed almost to have been struck dumb since they had entered the customs shed, only nodded her head vigorously.

'And you plan on being in Istanbul how long?' he asked.

'Only for one night. Or two at the most,' Gemma said. 'We're here to meet some friends who are on a camper trip. It depends how long it takes us to make contact with them. Let's say two nights to be safe.'

'And have you made a hotel reservation?' the colonel asked, unsmiling.

'No,' Gemma said; and then, more brightly, 'Could you recommend something?'

'The Hilton,' he said, so quickly that it seemed it must already have been decided, at least in his mind. 'Everyone there speaks English, which will be more convenient for you. And for one night, two at the most, it will not be too expensive, I think,' he said, still without a smile.

'Even for one or two nights, though, that's too rich for my blood,' Gemma said. She fumbled in her purse and found the tattered guidebook she had purchased in Athens for mere pennies. It was several years old, but streets didn't change names, she had decided. She opened it to a well-marked page and pointed to a hotel listing she had underlined in red ink. 'We thought maybe this one.'

He took no more than the briefest of glances at the listing and shook his head firmly. 'That one is out of business,' he said, 'I regret to say.'

'Oh . . . ' She had not anticipated that. It was true, streets did not often change names, but hotels might come and go overnight, something that had not crossed her mind when she purchased the book.

'I will arrange for a guide,' he told her in the tone of voice that brooked no quarrel. 'He will help you find a hotel room, whatever you need. Thomas,' he called over his shoulder.

'Oh, but we can't afford a guide,' Gemma started to say.

'He will work cheap,' he forestalled her

objections. 'Very cheap. Say, three dollars a day.'

Thomas had come in through the same door the colonel had used earlier. He seemed to be a smaller and younger (eighteen? Nineteen? Surely, Gemma thought, no more than that) version of the man before them, perhaps even his son, with the same dark eyes, but with a bright smile already in place.

'Ah, young ladies, you will come with me, I will see to everything,' Thomas greeted them, even making a slight bow, as if these things had already been decided. As perhaps, she was thinking, they had been, although she and Marianne had had no part in that decision.

Gemma, realizing that three dollars a day was not very much and might even end up saving them much more than that, decided that resistance was not only futile, but might prove costly in the long run. She said to the smiling and eager-looking young man, 'Right now, what we need is a hotel. Maybe you could help us with that.'

'Umm.' He seemed to consider the

matter carefully for a moment, before his face brightened and the wide smile came back. She felt sure she knew beforehand what he was going to say. 'The Hilton, I think,' he said. *Bingo*, she thought.

'No, we can't afford that,' she insisted. 'We were thinking more like one of these listed here.' She raised the guidebook in the air.

He didn't even so much as glance at the book. 'No, no, those places are not suitable for such fine young ladies as you. American young ladies, yes?'

'Yes,' Gemma said. Although she had the impression he had known this before he asked.

'I thought as much,' he said, beaming at her. 'May I ask, young miss, how much had you planned to spend?'

'Well . . . ' Gemma hesitated. Did people here haggle the way they did in some countries? Or not? No one had ever told her. 'We were thinking maybe twenty U.S. dollars a night.'

He screwed up his face, calculating. 'So, maybe sixty lira.' He waggled his fingers to indicate that the figure was only an estimate. 'It is not much, mademoiselle, for a good hotel room in Istanbul. This is a major city, you understand, a great city.'

'Yes, I know. But we don't need anything fancy,' she said. 'Just beds, and if possible, a bath. It's only for a night or two.' She gestured once again with the battered guidebook. And again he ignored it completely.

'No, no, it is all right, you are not to worry,' he insisted. 'Thomas will take care of everything, you will see. I have a cousin — he works at the Hilton, at the check-in desk. I will call him on my cellphone, see.' He took the phone from his pocket and showed it to her, as if she might be questioning its existence. 'I tell him we can pay no more than sixty lira, tops. Maybe seventy?' He lifted an eyebrow at her. 'If sixty is not possible?'

'Yes, seventy, certainly,' she agreed. 'We can do that if we have to. But do you really believe we can . . . ?'

'It is settled, then,' he said, looking entirely pleased with their transaction. 'Please, come with me. I will take care of everything. Give me your bags, if you will. We will go in my car. You see, you will have no taxi fares to pay. Those taxi people are thieves, every one of them. Worse than pirates.' He shook his head fiercely, as if sorely vexed by the city's taxi drivers. Then he smiled brightly again, once more revealing rows of gleaming teeth. 'You see, young ladies,' he said cheerfully, 'already Thomas is saving you money.'

* * *

As it happened. Thomas's cousin was indeed able to get them a double room at the Hilton for sixty lira a night. A room, Gemma thought, casting her eyes about the room when they had been shown to it, surely worth more than that paltry figure.

'Gemma, look,' Marianne called from the bathroom where she had gone first thing, 'we've got a tub *and* a shower.' There was the sudden loud gush of running water. 'Oh, and the water's good and hot. I'm going to soak for an hour, I

129

swear; you'll have to drag me out of the tub by my hair.'

Not until the two young ladies were actually ensconced in their room, with Marianne already filling a tub with loudly running water, did Thomas allow himself to call Ben Craig on his cellphone.

'I have made good the difference with the hotel,' Thomas said, 'as you instructed. But really, how could those two possibly believe even for a minute that they would get a room at the Hilton for sixty lira?'

'They're not seasoned travelers,' Ben said. 'And don't worry about the money. You'll be reimbursed. How do they seem?'

'The brunette seems a little ... ' Thomas paused to think. 'A little tired, I believe. I think she did not sleep well on the trip here.'

'But it's nothing serious, I hope?'

'No, I do not think so,' Thomas assured him.

'And the blonde? Gemma?'

'Ah, the blonde.' Thomas's eyes sparkled wickedly. 'She is a bundle of energy, that one. And so beautiful. She will make some man a fine mistress.'

'Not you, sorry to say,' Ben told him sharply, sounding not at all sorry, 'so put those thoughts out of your head right now.'

'Of course. I do not want you to think . . . ' Thomas stammered, stunned by the other man's vehemence. 'I am a businessman. An honorable businessman. I do not take advantage of my clients. I would not want you to think so.'

'I understand,' Ben said in a more conciliatory voice. 'I just wanted to be sure we were clear on that. The people paying for all this aren't interested in financing your love life. Even your fantasies, as far as that goes.'

'My . . . ? I do not know that word.'

'Never mind. Just keep everything aboveboard. Did they indicate where they might be going?'

'I am to pick up Miss Gemma at one o'clock,' a greatly subdued Thomas said. 'Her friend has decided she will stay at the hotel. But Miss Gemma wants to see the seraglio.'

Meaning, Ben thought, the Sultan's

seraglio. A perfect place, it seemed to him, for a meeting. And if Gemma was to be alone, that was even better.

* ★ ★

Ben's local friends, still working in Turkish intelligence, had been happy to meet with him and hear what he had to tell them.

'These two young men,' Fahri, the Turkish agent in charge, said. 'Are they smuggling drugs, do you suppose?'

'I think it's unlikely, though they might be using them,' Ben replied. 'And I don't think they're the ones calling the shots. I think that's a man called Ralph.'

He had figured things out while killing time in that isolated motel in Greece. If he remembered that old file correctly, Ralph was Reidl's handler. Once he had remembered that, it was clear where all this was heading. He already knew that the two young men were paying visits to various Russian cells and terrorist groups, many of them Russian vassals; giving them support, perhaps even monetary

132

support, hatching plots, coordinating all with his handlers. And a camper full of students had provided perfect cover for his mission. That much of their activities he was glad to share with Turkish intelligence, as they were glad to receive his information.

And most likely in time, Gemma would become a hostage. Perhaps, without her realizing it, she already was. Once she had been handed over to Ralph, however, he could use her to exert pressure on David Dolan, who was one of the best-connected men in Washington. The whole trip had been intended, perhaps, to give Gemma time enough to fall in love with the infamously seductive Kurt Reidl, aka Kevin Norton. But that possibility Ben kept to himself. He was convinced that, their trip finished, the two young men intended to deliver Gemma to their handler in the U.S. He had determined that he would somehow get Gemma out of there before that happened. But to do that, he would almost certainly have to share his convictions with Gemma's father.

Getting her away from those two young men was the least of it. If need be, he could do that by force; and if that was the only way, then he was prepared to resort to that, even knowing that Gemma would surely never forgive him for doing so. But the Russians, in his opinion, had long memories. If Gemma was ever really to be safe, Ralph too would have to be dealt with.

And to accomplish that, he would need help. High-powered help.

13

Craig was in the second courtyard of the seraglio that afternoon when he saw them walking toward him through the plane trees — Gemma and her young guide, Thomas. He hurried out to meet them, waving his hand. She stopped dead, staring at him in disbelief.

'Ben Craig,' she said. 'This *cannot* be just another coincidence. Are you following me?'

'Sort of. Except I was here first,' he pointed out. 'No, I wanted to see you. I need to talk to you. Thomas, do you think you could wait for us over by the gate?'

'I will bring my car around. It will be waiting,' Thomas said, and was gone, all but running for the gate.

'You said you wanted to talk to me. About what?' Gemma's eyes narrowed suspiciously. 'This isn't something my father's cooked up, is it?'

For a second or two, Ben was tempted

to tell her; but he had given his promise. 'No; I swear it was my idea alone.' Which was, in a sense, the truth. 'But you must realize,' he added solemnly, 'that I don't need anyone to tell me to keep an eye on you.'

'Thanks, that's very flattering to hear. I'm grateful, I really am, but I don't honestly think I need anyone keeping an eye on me, as you put it,' she said in a firm voice; but then her eyes widened as she realized something. 'Oh, I just thought — Mr. Dragoumis, on our ship. That wasn't a coincidence either, was it, him showing up like that and being friendly?'

He gave her a sheepish smile. 'You're right, he's an old friend of mine. And I didn't exactly ask him. When I told him about your plans to take that freighter to Istanbul, he offered to keep an eye on you, for the first part of the trip at least. His home is on Lesbos. That's why he left the ship there. I'm sorry he couldn't go the whole way with you. He looks harmless, but believe me, he's not.' He started to tell her about the crew member who had been watching over them for the second leg of the trip, and thought better of it. If she had not liked being protected by Alexei Dragoumis, she was certainly not going to be pleased to know that some probably ill-bathed sailor had shared the job with him. And he was painfully aware that already he was skating on thin ice.

'We were fine, thanks to his coaching,' Gemma said. 'But I repeat, I do not need anyone to keep an eye on me.'

Oh, but you do, he thought, and did not say. 'Your friends,' he said instead, 'in the camper — have you caught up with them yet?'

'No; they were planning on staying in Bursa. It's near here, I think.'

'Bursa? That's right, it's close by. But Gemma, when we talked before, you said the plan was to head from Turkey to India.' She nodded. 'Do you understand that means driving across some of the most dangerous terrain on earth? Iran, Afghanistan, Pakistan?'

'Kevin says we'll be safe,' she said.

'And you trust him, do you?'

'On that subject, yes, I do,' she said, and added quickly, 'Even if it's because I know he'd want to save his own bacon.'

And I must not make the mistake of underestimating this young woman, Ben thought. They were to be safe? The Russians must be calling in a lot of chits if they could make that sort of guarantee. Of course, Norton, alias Reidl, was not just a Russian operative. He was a terrorist as well, and those groups had their own code of honor. They tended to look out for one another. So perhaps after all it would be safe for the little camper. It was not necessarily safe for her, though.

'I got the impression you haven't been having much fun,' he said, trying another approach. 'In that case, may I ask why you're so determined to continue with this trip?'

She gave him an arch look. 'Let's just say I'm curious.'

'About what?'

'About a lot of things. About Kevin Norton's odd interest in me, for one.'

'Oh I'm sure he's interested in you, in a few ways,' he said. 'That's not hard to figure out.'

'But it is,' she insisted. 'All this time,

and he hasn't hit on me once. Don't get me wrong; I'm not saying I want to have to fight him off. It's just that he keeps saying things that make me think he likes me, but I don't see that in any of his actions.'

'Maybe he's just shy,' Craig suggested. 'Some men are.'

'Shy?' She snorted her disdain. 'You don't know Kevin Norton,' she said. 'He's about as shy as a barracuda.'

A good description for the man, Ben thought. Kevin Norton was indeed a barracuda, and just as dangerous. Gemma Dolan did not even know she was swimming in infested waters.

'And after India?' he asked her. 'Have they made any plans beyond that?'

'Nothing concrete yet. Kevin said he'd like us — the two of us I mean, him and me — to fly back to America. His Uncle Ralph has been financing him on this trip, and now says he'd like to meet me.'

I bet he would, Craig thought. 'Uncle Ralph' had been financing more than his nephew's trip; he had been financing a pack of terrorist cells, too. 'He's taking you home to meet the family?' he asked aloud. 'Have things got to that point between the two of you?'

Gemma gave a little chuckle. 'No, but I bet he'd like to think so.'

For a moment, Ben again considered telling her everything; forbidding her, in her father's name, to go any further. But the sad truth was, he doubted that short of physically restraining her, he had any hope of preventing her doing as she pleased. Things might, in time, come to that, but he was not yet ready to risk everything on that course of action. He would do whatever he had to do to keep her safe, but his every instinct told him she would never forgive him if he used physical force against her. And that possibility brought him nothing but grief.

Which left him, really, only one alternative: to do exactly as he had been commissioned to do, which was to keep her safe. And if that meant following her across hell, well, then so be it. If their little group was safe navigating those treacherous waters, a single man following in their wake was probably going to be safe as well. By the time anyone noticed him, he was going to be already past the danger. Anyway, thanks to his contacts here, he might not have to follow them personally. Turkish intelligence had been very interested in what he'd had to say about terrorist activities. He intended to keep them well informed.

He and Gemma had been walking through the seraglio as they talked, and now they had reached the first, mostly empty, courtyard.

'This,' he said, gesturing around them, 'was where the Janissaries were stationed. You've heard of them, I suppose.'

'Yes, but I don't remember much about them. Warriors of some kind?'

'They were the sultan's personal bodyguards, and probably the fiercest warriors ever.'

'Turkish, I bet.'

'They were used by the Turks, as bodyguards to start with and later as sort of a commando force. But no, they weren't Turkish originally. For the first hundred years or so they were Greek — tribute children, actually, taken forcibly as tots by the conquering Turks and turned into savages. Blond Greek boys were in demand here at that time, as you can imagine. For years the Janissaries terrorized Europe for the Turks, including their original Greek homeland.'

'It's hard to think how they could be trained to turn against their own people,' she said.

'Not that surprising. Modern-day terrorists do the same thing,' he said, wondering if she would make the connection. But of course, she did not know about Reidl, the terrorist. To her he was still Kevin Norton, footloose young American who wanted to take her home to meet his benevolent uncle.

Somehow he had to prevent that. Once she was caught in Uncle Ralph's web, there would be no escape for her. Not while she was alive, certainly. Whatever they might promise up front, terrorists did not work that way.

So, yes, she was indeed probably safe for the duration of the trip, as Kevin Norton had promised, though he intended to keep an eye on her nonetheless.

142

Once, however, she had been delivered into the hands of the mastermind behind this scheme, she would be forever at his mercy. That he had to prevent at all costs, even if he had to forcibly kidnap her.

'And they were just children to start,' he added. 'Children are malleable.'

'Poor little things,' she said, shaking her head sadly.

'Thank you.'

'For?' She looked surprised.

'For caring. Not everyone does.'

They had reached the main gate, and there just past it was Thomas, waiting with the rear door of his car standing open.

She held out her hand. 'Ben, thanks so much for showing up this way. But don't worry about me, please. I can look after myself. I promise.'

He took her hand in his and, raising it, gently kissed the tips of her fingers. 'I have my own reasons for worrying. And when are you meeting your friends, by the way?'

'I left a note for Kevin with American Express. He's supposed to meet us tomorrow at the Hilton. If he's not still mad at me.'

'I have a feeling he'll have gotten over it,' Ben said drily.

She laughed and, leaning close, surprised him with a sudden kiss. Not on the cheek, either, but on the lips. But by the time he might have grabbed her in an embrace and made something more of it, far more, than a quick peck, she had twisted away and, with another laugh, this one of delight, run across the pavement to Thomas's car. She waved once as Thomas closed the door, and then they were gone, swallowed up in the endless river of Istanbul's traffic.

Long after they had vanished, Ben Craig remained where he was on the pavement, staring after them. Then with a melancholy sigh, he turned and started for his own car.

Oh, Gemma, Gemma, he thought with a sad shake of his head.

14

Gemma arrived back at the Hilton to discover Kevin already there waiting for her, though the arrangements had been that he would meet them there the next day in the afternoon.

'Aren't you a little early?' she asked him. Marianne, as she could see, had already packed her things. Obviously the two of them had been waiting for her to return.

'I had some business in the city today,' he said, pretending not to notice her annoyance, which only annoyed her all the more. 'I didn't see a point in making the trip in twice when I could pick you up today.'

'And what if we don't want to leave today? Maybe we want another day in Istanbul.'

'For what?' he asked suspiciously.

'For . . . ' she said, and floundered. 'For one thing, Marianne's been feeling sick.'

'Gemma, I'm fine, really I am,' Marianne said quickly. 'I just needed a good rest after that boat trip. Besides, to tell you the truth, I'm looking forward to seeing everyone again.'

'Seeing Walt, you mean,' Kevin teased her.

Marianne blushed. 'Well, yes. Of course. Him too.'

And I think I know why, Gemma thought. 'Plus there were sights I wanted to see before leaving Istanbul,' she said aloud.

'There are plenty of sights to see in Bursa,' he told her. 'That's where we're camping, in case you forgot.'

'I'm sure there are things to see there, but it isn't the same.'

'How would you know, if you haven't seen them?' he asked. 'Come on — I have a rental car, and it's costing me a fortune. It's sitting at the curb outside, but I don't know how long it'll wait.'

'We hired a guide,' Gemma said lamely. 'He was expecting two day's work.'

'No problem. I'll pay him for the extra day.'

'No, you won't. I'll pay him myself,' Gemma insisted. 'And I'll write him a note to explain.' Before he could object, she went to the writing desk against one wall and wrote a quick note to Thomas. Enclosing the extra day's pay with it, she slipped both into one of the hotel's envelopes.

'Where is he, this guide of yours?' Kevin asked, eyeing the note in her hand. 'I want to meet him. I know these Turks, the ones who rent themselves out like that. I'll bet he's a letch, just waiting for a chance to get you two alone.'

'He's not; he's really sweet. And he's probably waiting right now in the lobby. I told him when he left me just now that I'd come back down in a few minutes. But I'll have to pack first.'

'We've already done that for you,' Kevin said, and when she looked astonished, he added, 'Marianne helped me. We thought it'd save time. The rental car, remember?'

Though she was inwardly seething at the presumption, Gemma could see that she was outnumbered. And with her eyes, at least, Marianne was pleading with her. She thought the best course of action was to go along with the other two, for the moment anyway.

'Okay,' she said, 'let's go find Thomas.'

Kevin hoisted her already packed duffel bag. 'I'm looking forward to it.'

As expected, Thomas was waiting for her in the lobby. His eyes widened when he saw the trio emerge from an elevator.

'I'll take care of that,' Kevin said, indicating the envelope in Gemma's hand.

'Never mind, I'll do it,' she told him. 'If you want to be helpful, you can talk to someone at the desk. The room's already paid for, so it won't cost you anything but your time, and hardly any of that. All you have to do is give them this.' She thrust her room key at him and swept past him to hurry to the waiting Thomas.

'It looks like we're leaving earlier than we planned,' she said, putting the envelope in his hand. 'I've paid for your lost day.'

'You did not need to worry about that . . . ' he stammered.

'And I wanted to thank you for taking

148

care of us,' she said. She leaned close to give his cheek a kiss, which gave her the opportunity to whisper, 'Please, will you let Mr. Craig know?'

By the time she leaned back from a blushing Thomas, Kevin was already there. How on earth, she wondered, had he managed things so quickly at the front desk? Her every interaction with the people at that desk had taken forever.

Kevin extended his hand to Thomas. 'And I want to thank you too, for looking after our ladies. They're precious cargo to us, as I'm sure you understand.'

'Yes, sir, I do,' Thomas said, shaking his hand and still blushing.

Kevin took Gemma's elbow in a proprietary manner. And with that, they exited the Hilton's lobby, Marianne following dolefully behind the other two, and carrying her own duffel, although Kevin still had Gemma's.

★ ★ ★

Try though she might, Gemma could not really feel good about rejoining the group, although she could see that Marianne was happy, and, after a quick visit inside the camper alone with Walt, she seemed to have recovered from her bout of ennui.

Part of the problem, Gemma had to admit, was with Kevin. It sometimes seemed to her as if all that she and Kevin did anymore was quarrel, especially since her return. Yet he was always so quick, the first one, to sue for peace. Was that because he really was sweet-tempered and good-natured, the easygoing young man he seemed to be? In which case, there was no use in pretending to herself — she really and truly was a bitch.

Or was he only patronizing her, trying to keep the peace for everyone's sake, including his own? She honestly did not know which. Or maybe it was a bit of both? That thought was not terribly comforting either.

Since their stay at that desolate beach in Greece, Walt had been giving everyone 'malaria' shots daily

'But there are no mosquitos here. Isn't that how malaria is spread, by mosquitoes?' Gemma had argued, but no one seemed to have heard her.

So far as she could discern, the only result of these daily shots was that everyone now laughed a great deal, even when, in Gemma's opinion, nothing was funny. Or they slept, sometimes the entire day through, waking only to get their next shot. In one sense, at least, Walt was proven right: no one had yet contracted malaria.

'I never knew fighting malaria was so enjoyable,' Marco said, and the others laughed with him. Which, Gemma thought, proved something, although she was not yet prepared to say just what.

Gemma herself was the lone holdout, the only one not taking the shots. 'I hate syringes and getting shots,' she said when Kevin brought the subject up. They were in the camper, driving. 'I even hate taking aspirin. And I feel as healthy as a horse, so why should I bother?'

'Still, if you did get sick, you'd infect everyone,' Kevin said. 'We're living in close quarters, you know.'

'Well that's true,' she agreed. 'But I won't get sick. Don't worry about that, because I never do. Anyway, if I wanted a shot I'd go to a real doctor, not Walt.'

'Walt was a medical student, so he knows what he's doing. And the vaccines were provided by a legitimate medical source, in Greece, while we were there. So you don't need to worry about that.' A Russian medical source, to be sure, but he did not tell her that.

'I'm not. Isn't that Russia over there?' she asked, pointing out the window at the distant mountains and changing the subject abruptly.

He blinked, astonished. It was almost as if she had read his mind, known what he was thinking. But of course that was not possible. He looked where she was pointing. 'I think so,' he said cautiously. 'Why?'

They were in Iran, heading for the city of Tabriz, where she had been promised they would be staying in an honest to goodness motel instead of camping.

'I was just wondering.' She looked back at him. 'Do you speak any Russian?'

'Me?' He looked astonished by the question. 'No, not a word. Why? Were you planning a visit?'

'No, not really. But we're so close that I can't help thinking it'd be a good idea if one of us did, just to be safe.'

'Safe? You think they're going to come over here, just swoop down on our little camper and, what, kidnap us all?'

'I don't know. Bad things happen sometimes. And the Russians . . . '

'What about them?'

'They don't always play by the rulebook, do they?'

'That's ridiculous.'

'Maybe it is. I'm just saying what I've heard.'

'What you've heard is ridiculous.'

She gave him a cold look. 'Yes, you said that already.'

'I suppose you might have a point,' he said, trying to patch things up. 'Well, if they do swoop down on us, as you seem to think, I'm sorry but you won't be able to count on me for much, not if it involves speaking Russian. I know English, if a bit imperfectly, and a smattering of French, a few words and phrases in Italian, but that's about it. What on earth made you ask me about Russian?'

She shrugged. 'No reason, just wondering again.' She looked out the window of the van. 'As far as that goes, I'm also wondering, by the way, if this is really safe.'

'This?'

'Going through Iran, I meant. This is Iran, isn't it?'

'Iran?' He looked out at the desolate landscape as if he had not seen it before, though they had been traveling through it for two hours or more now. 'Yes, it is. Why? And please don't tell me you were just wondering.'

'But I was. Besides, I thought they didn't like Americans here.'

'They make exceptions for students,' he said. 'Most countries do, believe it or not.' And, though he could not very well explain this to her, he had been promised all kinds of protection while they crossed this country; there were half a dozen cars following them along this highway, and he felt certain that some of them, at least, were meant to be a protective escort. 'Anyway, we aren't the only ones traveling through Iran. In case you didn't notice,

154

there are other cars on this road.'

'Yes. I saw you walk back when we were stopped at the last border crossing, to check everyone out. Did you find anyone interesting back there?'

He reminded himself again not to take this young woman for granted. She did not miss much. He had not even been aware that she had seen him stroll back to look at the other cars and their inhabitants. And, yes, it had been to check them out. Maybe Walt was right, maybe he should try again to persuade her to take the shots. Though that was probably a futile effort. So far she had given no indication of changing her mind. And, since that incident in Greece, he had been reluctant to talk to Walt about Gemma at all.

'I didn't find anyone interesting, no,' he answered her. 'Two Turkish men in one car; carpet buyers, they said. A Swiss family on vacation, though this seems an odd choice for a vacation trip.'

'But *we're* here,' she said quickly.

He ignored her comment and continued, 'Some Australian jocks in a flashy red sports car; a Jaguar, I think it was. There was even a pair of Iranians, believe it or not. Oh, and a single man traveling alone, from here in Iran, but I've forgotten where he said he was from. I think he'd been on vacation in Turkey.'

Any of whom, he was thinking, could be the protection he had been promised. Except, of course, for the Australians. No operative drove around in a flashy sports car. It attracted too much notice.

'My point was,' he finished his summation aloud, 'if any of them thought it was dangerous, they wouldn't be here either, would they?'

'Unless they didn't know it was dangerous,' she said.

'Meaning they're stupid, and only Gemma's got a brain — is that what you're trying to say?'

'Being curious isn't the same as being smart,' she said angrily.

He thought it safer to change the subject. 'That way,' he said, pointing off to the right, 'is Kurdish territory. There's lots of fighting over there, which means that, yes, going that way would certainly be dangerous. But I'm sure we're safe here, as long as we stay on the main highway. I don't think this a spur-of-the-moment kind of society. Are you satisfied?'

'You said that about Greece, too.'

'What?'

'That it wasn't a spur-of-the-moment kind of society. Maybe that's what all the differences really come down to. Americans are used to doing things just because they feel like it. Here, everything has to be carefully scripted. It's kind of sad in a way.'

'I suppose that depends on who's writing the script. I guess you think you're qualified to do it.'

'Not me. Not anyone else's script, at least, but think I'm entitled to write my own.'

'Entitled? People always think that,' he scoffed. *At least*, he thought, *the bourgeois pigs think so.*

'You always sound angry when you mention 'the people',' she said.

'That's not fair, Gemma. Can you honestly say that a lot of those people you're talking about aren't silly and misguided?'

'Some of them are, I suppose,' she conceded.

And, she thought, he had done it again; turned things around until she was once more the foolish one. How did he always manage that? She had never before thought of herself as unreasonable, but somehow in their conversations that was how she always ended up sounding.

He put an arm around her waist and tried to draw her close, and noted her resistance. Walt was growing more and more uneasy about Gemma. If he did not keep her in line, another incident was almost certain to happen, and this time he might not be on hand to thwart it, though why he should want to, he was not clear on even in his own mind.

'It's not just the shots, either, though I'd be a lot happier if she was taking them like the others,' Walt had said the last time they talked about her. 'But she notices too damned much. That girl is too clever for her own good.'

'Don't worry about Gemma. I can handle her,' Kevin told him yet again. Walt only gave him a roll of his eyes and a smirk. That had been pretty much his standard attitude since Greece, since that odd rebellion on Gemma's part.

At least Marianne no longer was a problem. She had even stopped making eyes at Kevin and concentrated, if it could be called that, on Walt instead. Walt, and her daily shots. She seemed to have no interest in anything else. Kevin had encouraged her attentions to Walt, albeit to the man's displeasure. Displeasure however, that was expressed, of course, privately to him alone. In public, he seemed to welcome Marianne's flirtatious advances.

'That's all I need, some brainless bourgeoisie throwing herself at me,' he complained when he and Kevin were alone.

'She's still Gemma's best friend, and you worry all the time about Gemma, right?' Kevin said. 'Well, Gemma almost certainly tells her things. So if Gemma really had any suspicions about us, she would voice them to Marianne. Who, let us hope, would in turn share them with you. That is why you need to be nice to her.'

'I am,' Walt said.

'Maybe nicer. And, may I remind you, we are supposed to be using them as our cover. The two of us traveling all this way alone, it might raise suspicions, particularly when you consider the out-of-the-way places we have been visiting.'

'We've been going exactly where we were told to go,' Walt said in a sulk.

'I realize that. And I'm not blaming you. But my point was, no one is going to take much notice of a busload of students. They do this sort of thing all the time, young people, especially college students. They are the perfect cover for a trip like ours. That's why Ralph arranged it this way.'

'Speaking of whom,' Walt said, seizing upon that name, 'does he know about Miss Gemma?'

'Know what?' Kevin asked warily.

'How difficult she has been, for starters,' Walt said.

'I don't know that she has been particularly difficult.'

'She asks a lot of questions.'

'So far her questions have not amounted to much, in my opinion. And I tell you once again, if you are worried about her questions, play up to Miss Marker. She's the one Gemma would most likely talk to if she had any suspicions.'

'It seems to me we should not need Marianne Marker to act as an intermediary, should we? If Gemma Dolan had any suspicions, I should think that you ought to be able to get them out of her. Or are you losing your touch, hmm?'

'Losing my touch? I think not. Gemma and are close, and getting closer daily, if you have not noticed.'

But they were not in fact getting closer. He had not discussed it with Walt, but the two of them quarreled often; had quarreled rather heatedly in fact over her sudden run for freedom in Greece.

'It was stupid and dangerous,' he scolded her when he saw her again in Istanbul. 'Taking off on your own like that.'

'I'm used to doing things on my own, thank you very much,' she told him. 'In case you hadn't noticed, I'm not exactly helpless.'

'I *had* noticed,' he said with a chuckle.

'To tell you the truth, it's one of the things I admire the most about you.'

'And what are the others?'

'The others?' He gave her a blank look.

'You said the fact I'm not helpless was one of the things you admired about me, which implies there are other things. I just wondered what else.'

'It'd take too long to list them all. But it sounds suspiciously like you're fishing for compliments.'

'Hmm,' she said. 'If I am, maybe I'm having a little luck.'

'And speaking of the others, what about them?' he asked abruptly, ignoring her hint. 'I mean, the others in our group. Or don't they matter at all to you?'

'The others in our group? What did my leaving have to do with them? Marianne went with me, but the rest of them stayed behind. Your obedient sheep, it seems to me.'

'They aren't my sheep — or anybody's sheep, as far as I can see. And of course they stayed behind. They didn't have your special invitation to travel to Athens. In a car, with your special friend, Mr. Craig.'

'Who I hardly know, so please don't call him my 'special friend',' she said. 'And he *didn't* give me the invitation. I invited myself and Marianne along, if you want to know. He was nice about it, but I got the impression he thought I was being a pain.'

'Maybe, maybe not. He could've said no when you asked. Besides, if you'd gotten into any kind of trouble, it wouldn't have looked good for the rest of the group, would it?'

'But I didn't,' she said triumphantly. 'What kind of trouble did you think I was going to get into?'

'I heard they held you up at Turkish customs.'

'And how would you know that?'

He gave another of his frequent shrugs. 'I hear things.'

'So what if they did? They were waiting for someone to come who spoke English.'

'Now you're being naïve. Do you honestly think they'd have people working customs who didn't speak lots of different languages? Turkey's a major tourist destination. People go there from all over the world. Those men probably spoke English better than we do.'

'I . . . ' she stammered. But she had no answer to that charge. It was something she herself had puzzled over at the time. Why had those men kept her and Marianne waiting? Presumably they had been waiting for the colonel to arrive. But who was he, that colonel, and what had been his particular interest in them?

'They probably thought you were smuggling drugs,' Kevin went on, taking advantage of her sudden silence. 'Don't tell me that wouldn't have been a problem for the others.'

'I don't see why it should've been, unless one of them *was* carrying drugs. Or someone else was.' She gave him a challenging look.

'Well, no one is, as far as I know, so get that idea out of your head. Has someone been talking to you?'

'What do you mean, talking to me? And what someone? How could I talk to anyone, cooped up in our little van all the time? Anyone but you, I mean.'

'But you've not been cooped up in our

little van all the time, as a matter of fact, have you? You went AWOL for a week or more.' He gave her a suspicious look. 'Did you meet anyone while you were in Athens? That Mr. Craig of yours, for example; your friend from Florence. You rode into Athens with him, according to what Marianne told me. Did you spend your time in Athens together? Did you see him in Istanbul too?'

'Istanbul? We had a guide while we were in Istanbul, you know that. You saw him that day you collected us at the Hilton. He was a nice guy.' Reminding him of Thomas spared her the necessity of actually answering his questions. Apparently Marianne had not seen fit to mention that they had indeed spent much of their time in Athens in the company of Ben Craig. Luckily, for much of that time Marianne had seemed to be in some sort of daze.

And of course, the day of that surprise meeting with Ben Craig in the sultan's seraglio, Marianne had been back at the hotel, in bed. So of that meeting, and indeed of Ben's presence in Istanbul,

Marianne was ignorant. Meaning she could hardly have shared that information with Kevin. So unless he had been following her — and she doubted that he had, since apart from the Hilton, he would have had no clue where to find her — then Kevin remained ignorant as well of the fact that Ben had even been there. And certainly she had no intention of telling him about it.

And, though she felt guilty even thinking it, thank god Marianne had been feeling sick that day. Though she was beginning to suspect that she knew just what Marianne's 'sickness' entailed. She could only very much hope she was mistaken.

And, yes, Kevin was thinking, he did know about the guide. He had not only seen him in the hotel's lobby, he had even contrived an excuse to speak to him briefly, to thank him for taking care of the two young ladies. So, yes, he was just a kid, their guide; a tout of sorts, Kevin had decided. He had been maybe eighteen or nineteen years old, all pumped up over looking after two pretty girls; but except

166

for his vanity, Kevin had decided Thomas was harmless enough. He was the sort of bourgeois pig who had not a serious thought in his head. Only sex and money would mean anything to him. Kevin had known hundreds, maybe thousands, just like him. He had nothing but contempt for them.

While he was in Istanbul, Kevin had visited a terrorist cell there; had brought them an infusion of money, cold cash. As he understood it, the money was intended to finance one of their projects, a bombing they were planning at one of the big tourist hotels. Perhaps even the Hilton, for all he knew. A bombing in which Gemma's 'nice guy' might even die, one of the victims.

Kevin felt no remorse for him, or for any of the likely victims. People would die regardless of anything he did or did not do. If people like young Thomas died in some operation that he had helped plan or helped finance, it was no great loss, to anyone.

Not to him, certainly.

15

Any ideas Gemma might have entertained about their 'motel' in Tabriz were soon dashed, however. She had imagined something like one of the American chains, all spit and polish, bathrooms and televisions in the lobby and in every room, and a shiny dining room for their meals.

This was obviously a local inn, and not at all like what she had been imagining. Walt drove the camper along a dirt track that led to the rear. At least three of the cars that had been behind them on the road followed in his wake: the Turkish carpet buyers, the Swiss family, and the caboose in their little train, the Iranian couple. The Australians in the flashy sports car drove on; probably, she thought, they were looking for something a little better. She wished she could have driven past with them. Surely, even in Iran, there must be something better than this. The single Iranian man drove by too, but she thought he was probably aiming for home.

The ones who had stopped, like Walt, parked in the back, all but filling the little graveled lot, and the passengers exited their vehicles and trudged inside. There were no televisions to be seen in the lobby (which, Gemma felt sure, meant none in the rooms either) and there was only one bathroom, at the end of the hall and meant to be shared by all the guests, Kevin informed them when he pointed it out.

'Which means no long soaks in the tub,' Gemma sighed. 'I hope there's an actual toilet. Oh, wait,' she said when she saw his rueful expression, 'it's a hole in the floor again, isn't it, and the railings you hold on to so you don't slip, plunging yourself into more than despair.'

'It's rude to make fun of people's living standards,' Kevin chastised her. 'There's more to life than shiny bathroom fixtures.'

'And our sleeping arrangements? What about those?'

'We have three bedrooms in all,' Kevin

told her. 'You three ladies will share the first room along this corridor. The next is for Marco and Anders.'

'And the third?' Gemma prodded him.

At least, she thought, he had the good grace to look embarrassed. 'That'll be across the hall and down near the bathroom,' he said. 'Walt and I will share that one. Because,' he added quickly, 'we'll be up late. We have to go over some plans, including our future route, which it looks like we might have to reconsider. We'd keep anyone else in the room awake while we were talking.'

Dinner, in the dingy and ill-lighted dining room, was some kind of stew. Gemma was afraid even to ask what kind. Probably camel, she thought, and pushed it round disinterestedly on her plate, noting that Marianne only picked at hers too, as did Denise; but neither had been eating much of late, so that proved nothing.

After dinner, however, there was nothing for them to do except retire for the night. 'We might as well,' Kevin said, escorting Gemma to the door of her room, where Denise and Marianne had already retired, announcing with a show of yawns and stretches that they were ready for bed. 'We need to get an early start in the morning.'

At the door, he pressed the big old-fashioned metal key into Gemma's hand. 'As soon as you're inside, lock the door behind yourself and keep it locked. And no going out for midnight snacks or anything either. Stay here, inside, where you'll be safe. This isn't America, remember. Not even France. If these men see a woman wandering around in the dark on her own, there's no telling what might happen.' He did not mention the possibility of another attempt on her life, which would necessitate telling her things she did not need to know.

She felt guilty all of a sudden for being so quarrelsome with him, when he was so clearly concerned for her well-being. 'I promise,' she said, and rose on tiptoe to give him a grateful kiss. 'I'll stay right here. No adventures.'

A promise, as it turned out, that was easier to give than to keep. The three cots in the room the girls were sharing proved to be hard and uncomfortable, and the mattresses atop them were thin and stuffed with what she could only suppose was straw, because it keep scratching her arms and legs whenever she moved about.

Worse, the room was long and narrow with only one window high up in the short wall at the end, and despite the warmth of the desert night, that window was closed — not only locked, but barred — so that, short of breaking the glass, which she did not think was a welcome solution, there was no way for her to get air from that source. And, needless to say, there was no air conditioning in the room. None in the inn anywhere that she had seen.

By the middle of the night, Gemma was gasping for air and weary of listening to Denise, in the cot nearest hers, snore. She threw the single blanket aside and got up, slipping on her robe and feeling about in her duffel bag for the little travel flashlight she always carried with her.

She found it and switched it on, shielding the light with her fingers so as not to awaken the other two, though that seemed unlikely; both of them were apparently dead to the world. Probably, she thought, as a result of Walt's 'malaria' injections which, despite all efforts to persuade her otherwise, she had continued to refuse.

'This isn't malaria country,' she kept pointing out, though no one seemed to pay her any heed.

At the door, she hesitated. The enormous key projected from inside the lock where she had left it after following Kevin's advice to lock the door behind her. She remembered his warning, too, about going out after dark by herself.

In all fairness, she thought he probably was right, based on nothing more than the way that the two men behind the check-in desk had looked at the women in their group while they were registering. She certainly would not relish meeting either of them in the dark outside.

On the other hand, she felt sure she was going to go crazy if she did not somehow get some air. She turned the key slowly, carefully, so as to make no noise, and tugged the door open just wide enough to allow her to slip through.

In the corridor outside, she hesitated before locking the door again from the outside, and slipping the key into the pocket of her robe.

'Sorry, girls,' she whispered to the door. 'If the building catches on fire, I promise I'll brave the flames to rescue you, and this way at least you'll be safe from surprise visitors.'

She had intended to go for a quick stroll outside, thinking that even a warm night in the desert would be preferable to the room she had just left. But halfway to the outside door, the one that opened onto the parking lot in the rear, she thought again of Kevin's warning. Maybe, after all, it would be wiser to ask him if he would accompany her outside for even a few minutes. Surely his room must be as uncomfortable as hers had been. More than likely, he would welcome the invitation.

If, that was, the same idea had not occurred to him as well, maybe even sooner. She went along the hallway to the door of his room, lifted a hand to knock, and then brought it back down again. If Kevin were abed inside, and if she knocked, she would probably awaken not just him but Walt as well. She knew perfectly well how Walt would react if he heard that she wanted someone to accompany her outside. 'Go back to bed,' was the best she could hope for. 'And stay there,' probably to boot.

But, wait, she could hear the sound of voices from inside the room. Yes, there were two voices. Two men inside were talking low, too low for her to actually make out the words. Which meant, unless they'd had company, that both Kevin and Walt were still awake, since they were the only two assigned to that room.

But what company could they have had here, where Kevin had said they knew no one? She wished she had taken time to slip on her watch. It was surely two or three in the morning, she was certain of that much. Had some problem arisen that they were now thrashing out between them? He had mentioned a change of route. But that had been hours ago.

Surely that should all have been resolved in a few minutes.

She lifted her hand again to knock, and again brought it back down. Instead, she leaned her head against the crack of the door, listening. Yes, she recognized both their voices now, Kevin's and Walt's.

Only, she still could not make out the words. Not because they were speaking too low for her to hear, but because they were not speaking English. For a moment, she thought the two men inside were speaking German.

But it did not exactly sound like German either. Anyway, it *couldn't* be German, could it? Hadn't Kevin very plainly insisted that he spoke no German, way back at the beginning of their trip? Yes, she was sure he had, all the way back in Paris, as an explanation for why they could not take the direct route south, through Germany.

Apparently the two men inside were arguing about something, because they raised their voices just then and she heard one of them (That was Kevin's voice, was it not?) say very clearly the word '*nyet*'.

Nyet? That was Russian, surely, for the word 'No.' And Kevin had said as well, quite recently in fact, that he spoke no Russian. English, some French, and a few words in Italian. That was what he had told her, was it not?

The men in the room had once again lowered their voices. A chair scraped as someone stood. At almost the same time, she heard another sound, this one not within the room beyond but from somewhere, it seemed, further along the corridor. It had been so faint, however, that she could not readily identify it. It had sounded almost like someone closing a door stealthily.

Suddenly she was frightened. Was someone else abroad? Perhaps one of the employees of the inn, about to discover her in the hall in her night clothes, prowling about? This was Iran, after all. Women were definitely second-class citizens here — she had already seen that for herself while they drove — and who knew how they dealt with nosy women who weren't abed like they were supposed to be in the wee hours?

She decided after all that she would not knock at the door in front of her and ask either of them to go outside with her. Nor did she, in fact, want to be found alone in this dimly lit hallway, by anyone. Instead, she walked, almost ran, back down the hall, to the door of her own room.

★   ★   ★

Inside the room she had just left, Walt cocked his head to one side. 'Did you hear something?' he asked in English. 'I thought . . . '

'A door, maybe?' Kevin said. 'I thought I heard something too.'

'Might we have a snooper?' Walt said He reached down and took a gun from the open bag at his feet and checked that it was loaded.

'We will soon find out,' Kevin said. He got up and crossed quickly to the door of their room, opening it swiftly but quietly.

'No, there's no one here,' he said over his shoulder in a whisper.

Walt, who had followed him to the door, gun in hand, said, 'Funny, I would have sworn I heard something.' In fact, he had been hoping they would find Gemma Dolan outside in the hall. He had grown thoroughly sick of her incessant questions. He would be glad to put an end to her nosiness, and he had reason to think Ralph would be glad to hear of it. As for Kevin, well, it was his opinion that he had fallen in love with the girl. But Kevin was a loyal agent. In the end, he would do as he was told.

'We're probably just both spooked,' Kevin said, closing the door again and turning back into the room. 'And for the record, we should be speaking English, just to be safe. You never know when someone might overhear the wrong conversation.'

Down the hall, Gemma stood inside her darkened room, pressed against the door and holding her breath. She had barely made it back to her room in time, had only gotten inside before she heard the door to the boys' room opened and heard their whispered exchange.

The whispering voices faded again, as presumably Kevin and Walt went back into their room, and she heard their door close again, but quietly. Silence fell. Except, still standing at her door, she would have sworn she heard another door close somewhere nearby.

She stood listening for another long moment, but there was only silence outside. She decided she must have been mistaken. She let out the breath she had been holding and, taking the key, which now seemed to weigh tons, from the pocket of her robe, she again locked the door from the inside. Eschewing the flashlight, fearing that its gleam might somehow attract someone's attention, she felt her way through the darkness back to her bed.

While they had been in the hall, both Kevin and Walt had spoken English; she had heard them even though they had been whispering. But before that, she had heard what she had heard, and she was convinced she had heard them speaking Russian while they were inside their room.

Anyway, what did it really matter if it was Russian or German they had been speaking? Either way, it meant Kevin had lied to her — and not some innocent white lie, either, but one that could not be so easily dismissed. Why would he have felt it necessary to lie about the languages he spoke? And, even more tellingly, if he had lied about that, what else had he told her that was untrue?

It was still too hot to sleep, but she had lost all enthusiasm for a trip outside. Right now, she had things to think about.

Lots of things.

16

In whatever language the two men the night before had been arguing, it appeared by the next day that the subject of their argument had been their future route.

'Walt's made up his mind that we won't be crossing Afghanistan after all,' Kevin told her in the morning. 'It's too dangerous right now; there's a lot of fighting going on there. Instead, we're going to take the highway south and cross into Pakistan near Zahidan. It'll take us a little longer, and it means we'll be spending more time in Pakistan than we originally intended, but that's okay too. Compared to some of the other countries in this part of the world, Pakistan is a walk in the park. And just beyond Pakistan is India, so once we get to that border, we'll be on the home stretch.'

This was presented to the group, of course, as a fait accompli, no discussion allowed, although Gemma thought it unlikely that any of her companions would want to discuss this or any other matter in a logical and sensible fashion. They no longer seemed capable of any intelligent conversation.

She remained certain that what she had heard the night before had been Russian, and continued to wonder why Kevin had lied to her. But, it seemed, he was not the only one who had secrets. Ben Craig had tried to persuade her to leave the group, and it began to look now as if he knew things he had not told her. Perhaps she would have been wiser to do as he'd suggested, but she still could not relish the thought of leaving without Marianne, though she knew perfectly well that it might yet come to that. And this very morning, Marianne, admittedly somewhat dazed, had been clinging fondly to the arm of a not altogether happy-looking Walt Prescott.

Although it was only just after dawn, the camper outside was already idling, preparing for their departure. The entire inn, it seemed, was bustling with activity. The Swiss family, the carpet buyers, the

Iranian couple, everyone was going to and fro, carrying things out to the lot in back, to be deposited in their vehicles, and returning inside for more things to carry. And already the inn's staff was starting to look harried. Apparently people here liked to get an early start to their day.

'No breakfast?' Gemma had asked when Kevin had reminded her that time was fleeting, and he had given his head a shake.

'We'll come across something after a while,' he said. 'There are always people selling stuff on the side of the road, trying to make a few extra pennies. Maybe we'll get lucky and find some dates or fresh figs.'

Which, Gemma had to admit, would almost certainly be an improvement over anything that might come out of the inn's kitchen, if last night's dinner had been any indication of what to expect.

So an impatient-looking Walt was already seated behind the wheel of the idling camper, gunning the engine from time to time to show his impatience, while Kevin, having warned Gemma of the time, now waited at the van's open door to shoo everyone inside.

And Gemma dawdled deliberately, putting things into and pulling them out of her duffel bag at random, even knowing as she did so that it was both childish and futile. Delaying their departure for five or ten minutes was not going to do anything to change the circumstances.

But what was? She could not yet bring herself to think of leaving without Marianne, regardless of her present condition. Even if she had wanted to do that, and she was beginning to think that it might eventually prove to be necessary, how could she just leave anyway?

She could hardly just start walking down the road, even if she had any place to go, and Kevin was probably right about a woman traveling alone in this country. That was if she actually got anywhere, and she no longer thought that was likely. The two men in charge of their trip would hardly let her just walk away as if nothing mattered. For some reason beyond her comprehension, she was . . . well, she hesitated to think of herself as a prisoner, but in a sense that was exactly what she was. What all of them were, really, even if the others were enslaved only by chains of drugs.

Finally there was nothing more she could think to do to add to their delay. Carrying her duffel, she left the motel and started across the graveled parking lot. There was a small gray Fiat sitting just behind the camper, with two men standing by it. The Turkish carpet buyers, if she remembered correctly from Kevin's reconnaissance at the border. They had spent the night here at the inn as well, though she had no idea where their rooms might have been.

She thought of the strange sound she had heard last night, that might have been a door closing softly somewhere along the corridor. Had it been one of these two men? But why should they have been abroad? Or perhaps, like her, they had been stifling in their rooms. But as she walked toward the waiting camper and Kevin waiting none too patiently by its open door, she could not ignore the fact that the two carpet buyers were staring rather pointedly at her. As if they knew her. But that was ridiculous; they were perfect strangers. Weren't they?

As she crossed the lot, one of them, the one standing by the driver's door of their car, waved to attract Kevin's attention.

'Hello,' he called, pointing at the camper's rear wheels, 'it look as if you may be developing a, what do you call them, a flat.'

'What? No way,' Kevin said disbelievingly. He walked back to the rear of the van to see for himself. At the same time, the other carpet buyer moved quickly in Gemma's direction. Her instinct was to take a step back from him, to let him pass unimpeded; but before she could do so, he addressed her in a lowered voice.

'You are Miss Gemma Dolan, yes?' he said.

'Yes, I am,' she stammered, astonished that he should know her name; but he went on without actually waiting for her reply, speaking hurriedly.

'You are not safe here. If you want to leave, you may come with us now. Mr. Craig has asked us to look after you. We will keep you safe. Do you wish to come with us?'

'Ben? But . . . I . . . ' She was still stammering. She thought of what he had asked her, trying to marshal her thoughts into some kind of order. Yes, of course she wanted to leave. It was what she had been thinking about since last night's discovery. But how could she go, just leave, without Marianne, who was already aboard the van? Marianne, looking only half awake when she had exited their room, who had only looked blankly at her when Gemma had commented on how hot and airless it had been. 'I slept just fine,' she had said.

'No, I can't,' Gemma told the man before her. 'Not now, not yet, I . . . I just can't.'

'Then,' he said, thrusting a piece of paper at her. 'Mr. Rawamundi,' he said, still whispering. 'Call him at this number, in Delhi. He is a friend of Ben Craig's also. Whatever kind of help you need, he will see to it. But let no one else see that number, please.'

With that, he tipped his hat at her and

walked on by, in the direction of the inn. It had all happened so quickly that for a second or two she thought she might have imagined the whole scene.

But, no, there was that scrap of paper in her hand. She closed her fingers over it as Kevin once again strolled into view, some instinct telling her that she must not allow him to see it.

'It needs more air,' Kevin said, returning from his inspection of the tire, 'but it'll be okay to drive on until we can get to a station. What did he want?'

Gemma made a fist of her hand, crumpling up the scrap of paper. 'Who?' she asked blankly, giving him an innocent look.

'That man, the carpet buyer,' Kevin said. 'Didn't he speak to you?'

She followed his gaze to the carpet man's retreating back, as if seeing him for the first time. 'Speak to me? No. Oh, well, yes, he did say good morning, if that's what you mean. In surprisingly good English, by the way. And he tipped his hat as he went past. So I said good morning back. Why?' she challenged him. 'Am I not supposed to talk to anyone, or even to be polite?'

'There you go again,' he said with a laugh, 'talking as if you were a prisoner.'

But I am, she thought despairingly. Unless . . . the piece of paper in her fist almost seemed to burn her fingers. She clenched it tighter.

'Come on, get in,' he told her. 'Walt wants to get started. And he won't like hearing about that tire. I could've sworn it was fine yesterday.'

She wondered when the carpet men had let the air out of it. And if they were not really carpet buyers, what were they? They had mentioned Ben's name. The man who had spoken to her had said she would be safe with them. How could he say that unless he knew there was danger? Were they armed? Because instinct told her that either Kevin or Walt, or perhaps both of them, was. A week sooner, even a day ago, she might have thought that was ridiculous, but she was sure now it was not. Yet that man had told her she would be safe with them. What sort of friends did Ben have anyway? Who was he?

★ ★ ★

Inside, as they were turning onto the highway, Kevin took a seat directly behind Walt, and told him in a whisper about the low tire.

'It was fine when I checked it yesterday,' Walt whispered back without taking his eyes off the road. 'I always check everything over at the end of each day's drive. This is not a place where we would want to have a breakdown. So someone must have let some of the air out of it since then.'

'Why would anyone want to do that?' Kevin asked. 'There would be no logical reason to do so.'

'Maybe so he could have a chat with your girlfriend.'

'The Turk? With Gemma?' Instinctively Kevin looked over his shoulder, out the van's rear window. The car with the two carpet buyers had pulled out onto the highway shortly after them, but it had fallen back as the van accelerated. 'She said he only wished her a good morning.'

'It looked to me like a very lengthy

greeting,' Walt said.

A man with a camel walked along the side of the road. Walt gave them a wide berth as he went by.

★ ★ ★

In the car following them, Turkish intelligence agent Fahri had just finished his report, via his cellphone, to Ben Craig, miles behind them on the highway.

'She has Rawamundi's number at the Malabar in Delhi,' Fahri was saying. 'It was all I could do. She knows she can call there if she is in any danger.'

When the call had been disconnected, Ben drove in thoughtful silence for another mile or so before he reached a decision.

Gemma was in danger — he could no longer pretend otherwise. Yes, at his next stop, he would have to email David Dolan and tell him everything.

The time for action was fast approaching.

17

In Washington D.C., David Dolan paid a friendly visit to Roger McDonald, the deputy chief of the C.I.A. Dolan came bearing a lengthy report, which he handed first thing to the deputy chief.

'I think you'll find this interesting,' he said.

'I'll take a look at it.'

'I'd prefer it if you read it now, while I wait.'

'If you want. Pull up a chair.'

The two men sat on opposite sides of the desk. Dolan waited with ill-disguised impatience as McDonald quickly read the report.

'And this man,' Roger said, then paused to glance down at one of the sheets of paper, 'this Ralph Willoughby . . . ?'

'That's an alias. His real name is Lipp, Radnor Lipp,' David said curtly. 'You have a file on him as long as your arm. I've seen it.'

McDonald blinked behind his thick spectacles. 'Lipp? Yes, we do. I recognize the name. I don't even need to look it up to know you're right. But are you sure he and this Willoughby are the same person?'

'Ben Craig was your recommendation,' Dolan said. 'That's his information on your desk. Are you suggesting now that Mr. Craig isn't reliable?'

'Craig? Yes, of course, he's a good man, a fine agent. And he is nobody's fool. Is he the one who identified your Willoughby for you?' Dolan nodded. 'Well, then, I think we can accept that as a fact. But what exactly are you proposing we do with this information?'

'For starters,' Dolan said, 'I want my daughter safely out of this predicament she's landed herself in. Those two men, Prescott and Norton, can be arrested, can't they?'

'Yes, if what Craig says here is true,' McDonald said, thumping one finger on the sheaf of papers atop his desk. 'And he seems to have plenty of evidence — of money going to terrorist groups, for starters — so there'll be no problem with arresting them. And, just between us, I don't seriously think anyone's going to look too closely into how Craig gathered that evidence.'

'Why would they?'

McDonald gave a nervous little chuckle. 'Well, some of his methods might not have exactly been aboveboard. Never mind about that, though. I think several governments are going to love with what we've got to share. The only real problem I can see will be making sure your daughter's safe before we make the arrests.'

'That's imperative, of course. And what about this Willoughby, Lipp, whatever you want to call him?' Dolan said, leaning forward and resting his elbows on the edge of McDonald's desk. 'I don't like the idea of the little fish getting caught in the net while big fish stays in the ocean.'

'I don't think I'd exactly call those two schemers little fish. As for Lipp, let me think about that.' McDonald considered for a moment. Then he snapped his fingers. 'I'm being an idiot. It couldn't be easier. The bank accounts,' he said.

'What do you mean?'

'If he's using these two to funnel money to terrorist cells, he has to be supplying money to them somehow.'

'Rawamundi, with Indian intelligence, says he's got an appointment at a bank today to open an account in Delhi.'

''Yes, he'd need that, wouldn't he, if he's looking to start trouble in India. I think we can make that assumption. There are limits on how much cash those young men could be carrying on them at any one time, even if he trusts them implicitly, and the Ruskies are notorious for not trusting anyone too much.'

'They probably think everyone else is as underhanded as they are.'

'I'm sure they do.'

'This bank account in Delhi . . . '

'We'll be on top of that. And of course there must be other bank accounts, too. In Istanbul, say, and Amsterdam. Wherever they've made stops, I'd assume. If we can identify Lipp as the one opening the accounts, and Norton and Prescott as the ones making withdrawals, then we've got them. That's an international conspiracy. I don't think anyone in any of those countries would try to stop us from making the arrests. No one wants these crazies running around blowing things up, innocent people killed, damage done, not to mention making everyone nervous. On both sides of the pond.'

'All sides of it, as far as that goes,' David Dolan said.

'When it comes to that kind of trouble, we're all in the same boat these days, aren't we? Now if we can tie these men together with the bank accounts, and I'm sure we can, then we'll get them all behind bars, and fast. And for what it's worth, the laws in some of these places are a lot stricter than our own; their governments have suffered more from terrorism than we have. I'm willing to bet they're run out of patience for this kind of thing.'

'Then can I leave this whole business in your hands?' David Dolan got up from his chair. McDonald got up as well, and extended a hand across the surface of the desk.

'Don't worry,' he said. 'Indian intelligence is waiting to hear back from us. I'll call them right away. Thanks to you and Mr. Craig, we're about to put a lot of terrorists out of business.' He sighed. 'Unfortunately, there'll always be someone else to take their place. That battle never ends.'

'That,' David Dolan said, 'is your problem. My daughter's mine. And I want it solved. Sooner rather than later.'

'Yes, sir, I understand,' McDonald said.

David Dolan was known to have friends in high places. The highest, in fact.

18

When the group in the camper neared Delhi, it was to discover that the city and its environs were scorching hot.

'It's supposed to be the monsoon season here,' Kevin told them, 'but the monsoons don't seem to know that.' He took a dirty handkerchief to his sweating brow, and leaned toward the driver. 'Wasn't that our turnoff?' he asked in a whisper.

'Normally, yes,' Walt said. 'But I'm taking another route today.' He took the next exit and they were on a crowded city street.

'May I ask why?'

'If anybody is following us, they'll have a harder time of it this way,' Walt said. He turned a corner, and then another. The traffic outside the camper was nightmarish; cars, trucks, bicycles, even pedicabs all vied for right of way, weaving in and out, their drivers sometimes shaking fists and cursing at one another.

'Following us?' Kevin looked behind them. 'The carpet men? We left them behind long ago, I'm sure.'

'Somebody else might have taken their place. It's better to be safe than sorry.' Walt continued to dart in and out of the traffic, turning corners, following a torturous path through the busy city. Finally he pulled up in front of a decrepit apartment building. 'We're here,' he announced to the passengers.

'I thought we were going to stay at a hotel,' Gemma said.

'Apartments,' was all Walt said. He opened the door and jumped to the ground. 'Let's go, everyone.

Gemma looked at Kevin, who only sighed and shrugged his shoulders.

'Oh, well,' Gemma sighed, and shrugged too. She had made up her mind that this was where the trip ended for her. Whatever Marianne chose to do, she herself had traveled as long with these two as she intended to do. So what could it matter if she spent her last hour or two in a hotel or a ratty-looking apartment building?

'Which apartment am I in?' she asked Walt. He looked surprised by her docility.

'Three oh four,' he said. 'The door's unlocked, and the key should be in it. And you,' he addressed Kevin as he too clambered out of the van, 'come with me.'

Kevin followed him into the building's lobby. There was an old-fashioned cage-type elevator, with an Out of Order sign on it scrawled in English. They walked up the winding stairs instead.

'Is this wise?' Kevin asked as Walt used his key to open the door of their apartment above. Their original plans had been to stay at a cheap hotel locally. This building was owned by Russians, and except for a few more or less furnished vacancies, it was occupied by Russian operatives, active or retired. 'This place is probably pretty well known to anyone in the police or intelligence services. It's like waving a red flag, I should think.'

'Someone has been sniffing around,' Walt said. 'If they try anything funny here, we have plenty of backup to hand. Plus, in case you have forgotten, we have this also.' He went to the back door and threw it open, to reveal stairs descending into the darkness of an alley below. 'An escape route, in case we need it. Though I certainly hope we do not.'

'Please tell me the other apartments don't have the same back way out. Like the one that Gemma and Marianne are in.'

'They don't. Only this one. If anyone else wants to leave, it will have to be through the central lobby, with a few dozen pairs of eyes watching their every move. It's why I opted for this location instead of the hotel. And if we get any heat for it, I will take all the blame, so you need not worry. This was strictly my decision, and I will tell that to anyone who asks. Okay?'

'So long as my tail is covered,' Kevin said. 'For now, I have a meeting I have to attend. I should be back in two hours. If I am not, send the usual signals. It will mean I am in trouble. Send help.'

'Watch your step,' Walt said. 'My nose has been twitching all day.'

Kevin gave him a thumbs-up and left the apartment. Downstairs, he had just stepped out the front door of the building when a trio of uniformed police officers got out of a car at the curb and walked toward him.

'Kevin Norton?' the man in the lead addressed him.

'Yes?' Kevin took a step back, putting him once more within the building's lobby.

'I am afraid I must ask you to come with us,' the officer said.

'I don't understand,' Kevin said, his voice rising almost to a shout.

'You are under arrest.'

'Under arrest for what? There must be some mistake. Where are you taking me?'

'For international conspiracy to commit acts of terror,' the officer said. 'And please stop shouting, sir.'

The shouting, however, had served the purpose for which it had been intended. Inside the apartment Kevin had just left, Walt Prescott had heard the ruckus, had heard Kevin's shouted words. As he had planned all along, before the police officers had even taken Kevin away, Walt was running for the back door, for the stairs there. As he pounded down them, praying no one had yet been stationed in the alley outside, where an escape car would be parked, all he could think of was Gemma Dolan.

That bitch, he thought angrily. *This is her doing. I will see that she pays. She won't get away with this.*

*   *   *

'Gemma, please tell me you aren't serious,' Marianne said for perhaps the fourth time.

'I'm *totally* serious,' Gemma told her, stuffing the last of her things into her duffel. 'And for the last time, Marianne, I'm begging you to come with me.'

'Come with you where? You don't even know where you're going.'

'Away from here. Right now that's all that matters.' Gemma finished her 'packing' and zipped the bag up.

'Because some man who, let me remind you, you don't even know, gave you a phone number and told you to call it. And just because of that, you want to wander around in a strange city in a foreign country? What if it's a fake number? What if whoever it is turns you down when you call, or even laughs at you for falling for what was only intended to be a joke? What then? Do you honestly think you could just come back here and act as if nothing happened? Kevin and Walt might be dense, but they're not *that* dense.'

'I never thought they were. And as far as that phone number's concerned, if whoever I call can't or won't help me, then I'll call the consulate. Even better, I'll go to a hotel and call my father in Washington, and he'll make sure it's all taken care of.'

'Gemma, get a clue. You're halfway around the world from Washington.'

'And you think that'd stop him? There's nothing he can't do if he sets his mind to it. For both of us. We don't have to stay anyone's prisoners.'

'Prisoners? You've used that word before, but I can't see how you see either of us as prisoners.'

'I think we've been given the illusion of

freedom without, at any time since we left Paris, being free.'

'And I think you're imagining things.'

'If you're right,' Gemma said, 'then nothing will stop us from walking out of here right now. Marianne, I'm asking you one last time, *please* come with me.'

'I . . . ' For a moment, Marianne looked as if she were considering the possibility. But she gave a great sigh and pushed a wayward tendril of hair back from her face. 'I can't, Gemma. I just can't.'

Gemma looked long and hard at her old friend. Marianne's eyes were sunken now and ringed with black, her skin ashen. She had lost weight, so much that her once curvaceous body was now little more than a skeleton.

'No,' she said, sadly, finally admitting the truth that she had refused to face for so long, 'I suppose you can't.'

'Gemma . . . '

Gemma held up a hand. 'No, please don't say anything else. I think we've both said everything that needs to be said. Goodbye.'

'Then you really are going?'

Gemma made no reply, but simply picked up her bag and walked to the door. When she glanced back, Marianne was crying into her hands, but she made no effort to stop Gemma from walking out and closing the door behind her.

And now what? Gemma asked herself in the hall outside. She had noticed when they arrived earlier that there was a payphone in the lobby. That would be her first step. She had long since memorized the phone number she had been given, and torn the slip of paper into tiny shreds, which had gone done the hole in one of those infernal toilets in Iran.

But how did phones in India work? There was a group of men sitting in the lobby watching an ancient-looking black and white television. They eyed her carefully as she descended the stairs. 'Do any of you speak English?' she asked them.

'Yes, of course, miss,' one of them replied. 'We all do. You are English, then?'

'No,' she answered quickly. 'I'm American. And I wonder if someone could help me with the phone there.'

The one who had spoken to her earlier jumped up and hurried across to her. 'I will gladly do so, miss. What do you need to know?'

'Just the cost of a call,' she said.

'It is five rupees. I can change them for you, if you wish.' He dropped a hand to the pocket of his filthy trousers.

'No, I have some,' she said, fishing for the change in her purse. She had traveler's checks, too, at least three of them left. If she had to get a hotel room, she would need them up front, even if her father fixed everything later.

'Perhaps,' the man said, eyeing her closely, 'the young lady would like me to dial the number for her?'

She glanced at the phone on the nearby wall. It looked like an old-fashioned rotary dial. 'No, I think I can manage,' she told him. 'Would you mind depositing the coins for me? I don't see a coin slot.' She counted the rupees into his outstretched hand.

He hovered close as she carefully dialed the number she had memorized. There was nothing she could do about that other than turning her back on him and keeping her voice low.

Her call was answered on the first ring. 'Malabar Hotel,' an unfamiliar voice said. It was not, she was certain, her carpet buyer.

'This is Gemma Dolan,' she said, speaking distinctly. 'I was told to call here for a Mr. Rawamundi.'

'Yes, miss, yes,' the voice said excitedly. 'Mr. Rawamundi is away at this very moment, but I am Mr. Pataki, his assistant. He has been telling me that if you call, I am to do everything I can do to provide you with my assistance.'

'Oh,' she said, unsure of what she should do now. 'I think it might be best if I came there and waited for Mr. Rawamundi. The Malabar Hotel, you said?'

'Yes, indeed, miss. Shall I be coming to get you? If you will be saying to me where you are at this exact moment, I will — '

'No, no, I can't stay here,' she said. Even while they had been talking, she had kept one eye on the stairs, half expecting

Walt or Kevin to descend them at any moment. 'Just tell him I'll be there as soon as I can. And ask him, please, to wait for me.'

'I shall do so, miss, I assure you,' he said.

She hung up the phone. Her 'friend' still hovered nearby. 'Looks like I'll need a taxi,' she told him.

'They do not often cruise about in this neighborhood,' he said, looking sad.

Although the group watching the television had made a great pretense of ignoring her, one of them jumped up now. 'My brother has a car,' he said, coming to join them. 'He will take you wherever you need to go, the same as a taxi.'

'I want to go to the Malabar Hotel,' she said. 'I think it's near the docks.'

'That will be fifteen rupees,' he said. 'That is what a taxi would charge you for the same journey.'

'Fine.' She counted them into his outstretched hand. As she did so, she saw the man who had helped her with the phone dart out the front door. He seemed to be in a great hurry.

The car the gentleman took her to was an American Ford. The man and his brother had a conversation in some language unfamiliar to her. It sounded to her suspiciously like Russian. *And now you're being paranoid*, she chided herself. *Any foreign language you automatically peg as Russian.* What did she know of the Russian language, anyway?

Their conversation ended, the man from the lobby opened the door for her, and she slipped inside. 'The Malabar Hotel,' she told the man at the wheel.

'Yes, miss,' he replied, starting up the motor. The car moved into the stream of traffic. The driver glanced into the rearview mirror briefly. His passenger was sorting through things in her purse, so she did not see, as he did, her recent companion, his so-called brother, climb into a small gray car at the curb behind them. Nor did she see when the small gray car followed them into the stream of traffic.

American women, he thought with a smirk. *They are such fools.*

As he was being helped into the police car out front, Kevin Norton was smiling to himself. It was a damned nuisance, this being arrested, but nothing more than that. It looked as if his warning had been effective and Walt had gotten away. Two of the policeman had gone inside and had come back out alone, which surely meant Walt had made good his escape. Knowing Walt, he would have had contingency plans in place.

And Kevin had known since the night before that Ralph was already in the city. If Walt was still free, and it seemed he was, he would contact Ralph first thing. And as soon as he did so, Ralph, with his endless contacts everywhere, would see to everything. Probably, Kevin told himself as the car door was slammed shut behind him, he would be free before they had even finished the booking process.

★　★　★

At the Commonwealth Bank, some few miles away across the city, Mr. Garibaldi, manager of the bank, was in the process of finishing up some paperwork.

'If you will just sign these papers, Mr. Willoughby,' he said, 'we will be finished.' He pushed the paperwork across the top of his desk and handed his visitor a pen.

'And I now have an account with Commonwealth Bank,' Willoughby asked, scrawling his signature where it was indicated on the papers.

Mr. Garibaldi paused to look at the signatures Willoughby had appended to the documents. 'Yes, it looks as if you do,' he said.

'And the two young men whose names I have added to the account, they will be able to make withdrawals as they see fit, in the future?'

'That is so.' Garibaldi got up from his chair and started around his desk.

'But, wait, where are you going?' Willoughby asked, surprised.

'Only to the door, sir,' Mr. Garibaldi said. 'There are some gentlemen here who have been waiting to see you.' He opened his office door and two suited gentlemen entered the office.

'You are Mr. Ralph Willoughby?' the man in the lead asked.

'I am. And you are . . . ?'

'Sir, I am Mr. Gopal Rawamundi of the Indian Intelligence Service, and this gentleman is my deputy, Mr. Lavorti. I regret to inform you, sir, that we are coming to place you under arrest.' He made a gesture to the man behind him, who quickly produced a pair of handcuffs.

'Arrest?' Willoughby was incredulous. He looked around frantically. There was only one exit from the room, and the two men were blocking that. Garibaldi had retreated once again behind his desk, safely removing himself from the action.

The man with the handcuffs came nearer. Willoughby backed away as far as he could go, till his linen covered buttocks were pressed against the outer edge of Garibaldi's desk.

'This is unconscionable,' he cried. 'You have no right. I am an American citizen.'

'Then, sir,' Mr. Rawamundi said, and he looked genuinely saddened by this fact, 'you would probably have been wiser to have remained in that country, where I believe the laws against terrorism are not so strict as they are in India. But you are in India now, and so of course you are here subject to the laws of our country. Please, sir, I am afraid you must come with us.'

'I won't. You can't make me,' Willoughby cried, twisting away from the handcuffs.

'Ah, sir,' Rawamundi said, looking for all the world as if he were about to burst into tears at any moment. He glanced back at the open door and snapped his elegant fingers.

Immediately three uniformed police officers appeared in the doorway and advanced toward the man pressed against the desk.

19

Gemma exited the Ford at the front entrance to the Malabar Hotel, which looked, she thought, much like an American hotel. If she had to check into something to wait to contact her father, this was probably as good as anything else.

She went into the lobby and looked around. She had no clue how she was supposed to recognize either Mr. Rawamundi or Mr. Pataki. But Mr. Pataki had seemed to recognize her name on the phone, so perhaps they would know her when they saw her.

In which case, she need only wait for someone to approach her. She saw a news-stand across the lobby. Yes, that would be a logical place for her to wait. She went there and took a magazine off the rack, meaning to leaf through it. But as she glanced up, she saw an office door open nearby, and a small Indian man in a dark suit and with black hair glued rather closely to his scalp stepped out. He glanced around, saw her, and seemed to know who she was. He took a step in her direction. Instinct told her this must be Mr. Pataki. He had been watching for her, just as she had suspected. Perhaps he had even been given her description. Apparently there was more to Ben Craig than she had heretofore realized.

She started to return the magazine to the rack, but before she could do so, an arm came around her and a masculine hand seized her wrist in a firm grip.

'Miss Dolan,' Walt Prescott said close to her ear, 'What a surprise this is, running into you here like this. Meeting someone, are you?'

'No. What on earth made you think that? I was about to buy a magazine, that's all.' She caught Mr. Pataki's eye and gave her head a shake. He stepped back inside the door through which he had just come, though it remained open a crack. Meaning, she suspected, that he was watching what transpired in the lobby. She tried to tug her wrist free of Walt's grip, but he held it fast.

'You're lying,' Walt said. 'You made a call from our building to someone here. And you came here to meet whoever it was. Was it your friend, Mr. Craig?'

'Ben Craig?' She didn't even have to feign her surprise. 'What on earth would he be doing here in Delhi?'

'Meeting you, maybe?'

'That's ridiculous,' she cried. 'And let go of my wrist.'

'No, it isn't,' he said, smiling smugly. 'You called someone, and made arrangements to meet him here. Who was it, if not Craig?'

'No one. I just wanted to get out of that awful place, and this sounded like a good place to visit. I thought I'd have lunch here, in fact.' She gave her arm another tug. 'You're hurting me,' she said.

'Darling, you haven't begun to appreciate pain. But you will, I promise you that. Come with me.'

'Where's Kevin?' she demanded. She knew that Kevin was some sort of traitor too, but at least he had always treated her reasonably. She felt sure she could handle him.

'Kevin?' Walt actually laughed at her question. 'Where do you think he is, bitch? He's exactly where you arranged for him to be, under arrest.'

She was dumbfounded. 'Kevin, arrested? But . . . '

He gave her wrist another violent yank. 'And Ralph, too, I'm told. So don't give me any of your bullshit. I said come with me.' He gave her wrist another violent tug.

As if, she thought, she had any choice. He practically dragged her across the lobby, out the wide double doors, to a car waiting at the curb. But wait — weren't those two in the front seat watching as he dragged her up to the car, the same two who had helped her earlier? Of course; that was how he had known where to find her. They had led him right to her. She should have known. They had been altogether too eager to be helpful.

'Where are you taking me?' she demanded as he shoved her into the back seat and got in after her.

'Some place you won't walk away from so easily,' he said. He snatched her purse out of her hand and, opening it, helped himself to the traveler's checks and the loose change inside. 'And you won't be needing these anymore either,' he said, shoving them into his own pocket. He leaned toward the driver. 'Take us to the labyrinth,' he directed.

★ ★ ★

Rawamundi left the officers and his assistant to finish the arrest at the bank and returned outside to his waiting car. The driver opened the rear door for him and he slipped inside.

'Is it done?' Ben Craig asked from across the seat.

'Dear Mr. Willoughby is being arrested even as we speak. He will demand to speak to someone from the consulate, of course, but it will do him no good, you will see. Our laws are very clear on these matters, and very strict.'

'Then maybe we should go back to the hotel,' Ben said . . . 'There's still Gemma to take care of, and she might go back too. If not, we'll have to try to find her.'

Rawamundi leaned forward. 'The Malabar,' he instructed his driver. As he was leaning back in his seat, his cellphone rang. 'Ah, that will be Mr. Pataki from the Malabar,' he said, 'who may even now have news for us. Yes?' he said into the phone. He frowned. 'Yes, yes, I understand. How many of them were there? I see. No, do not fret about it, you did the right thing.' He put his hand over the phone and turned to Ben. 'I am afraid we will not have to search for the girl. At the moment, she is with Mr. Prescott.'

'What?' Ben fairly exploded. 'How did that happen? Pataki was supposed to be waiting for her to get to the hotel.'

'Indeed, but Mr. Pataki tells me that she had no sooner arrived there than Mr. Prescott showed up as well, and took her away again.'

'And Pataki didn't do anything to stop them?'

Rawamundi shrugged. 'He could do nothing, it seems. He followed the pair outside, but there were more men waiting in the car to which the gentleman took her. There were three of them in all, he tells me, and Mr. Pataki was not armed, so he could not stop them from driving away with the young lady. It is unfortunate, but we had no reason to suspect this might happen.'

Ben groaned and slumped back in his seat. 'Then we've lost her,' he said. And he would never work again, not after David Dolan got through with him. That was the one thing Dolan had insisted upon, that his daughter be kept safe. And now she was at the mercy of someone who, now that the plan to deliver her to his handler had fallen through, would not hesitate for a moment to kill her. He said as much aloud.

'Perhaps not,' Rawamundi said. 'And no, we have not lost her, not yet. Mr. Pataki could do nothing to stop them from taking her, that is true, but he is even now following their car.'

Ben's hopes soared. 'Tell him not to let them lose him,' he said.

Rawamundi smiled at him. 'Mr. Pataki has lived his entire life in this city. No one knows Delhi better than he, I can tell you that. They will not lose him.'

He went back to the phone. 'Yes, yes,' he said, 'and where are they now?' His smile vanished. He put his hand over the phone again and turned back to Craig. 'He thinks they are headed for the labyrinth,' he said.

'Is that bad?'

'Yes. Very unfortunate, I think. It is a bad quarter. A place where women, well . . . ' He hesitated. 'Her blonde hair . . . and I am told she is most lovely. She will be quite a prize there, I believe. Unfortunately, once a woman is sold into the labyrinth, she never again goes free.'

It took Ben a long moment to grasp what he was being told. 'Prostitution, you mean.'

'Slavery would be closer to the truth,' Rawamundi said. 'I said 'sold'. The people there, they buy them — women, young girls even, some of them mere children. After that, they own them. Body and soul.'

20

'Get out,' Walt ordered her.

The car had stopped. She was so surprised by his order that for a long few seconds she could only sit paralyzed. She had been convinced that he was going to kill her, and here he was telling her to leave the car.

'Where . . . where am I?' she stammered.

'Someplace you will never leave again.' He gave her shove. 'Out, I said.'

She stumbled out of the car, onto a broken sidewalk. For the moment, Walt did not have hold of her. In desperation, she began to run blindly, little knowing or caring where she was going, only that she was escaping from the man who had taken her captive.

Oddly, no one made an effort to stop her. She even thought she heard the other men in the car behind her laughing. She got to a street corner and looked frantically in both directions, but she had no idea where she was, or in what direction safety lay.

She looked at the building nearest her. Its front wall was made of glass, and beyond it she saw row upon row of women, some of them no more than children, staring at her. And some of them, too, were laughing at her. They were all in rooms the size of cages, and all the windows were barred.

At once, she knew. This was why Walt had not killed her. He had something in mind for her that was worse than death: a life without hope.

She sank in despair to her knees, and looked behind her. Walt was following, but not running, not even hurrying. He only trailed nonchalantly after her, smiling when he saw her look back at him.

Only, looking past him, she saw what he had not yet discerned: Ben Craig running hard toward them, and behind him an Indian man in a dark suit followed by a group of uniformed police officers. So hope was still alive after all.

Whether something in her expression

told him, or he finally heard the running feet, Walt suddenly realized something was amiss. He whirled about, at the same moment snatching a dagger from his pocket.

He was not in time, though. Ben was already upon him. He caught the hand with the dagger and bent it violently backward, forcing Walt to the pavement. There was a loud crack as something broke, and Walt gave a bleat of pain and terror.

The dark-suited man ran up to them then, breathing heavily. 'Ah, my poor dear Mr. Prescott,' he said, and sounded sad indeed, 'you have fallen and hurt yourself, I see. My friends here — ' At this moment, the uniformed police officers arrived as well. ' — will see that your injuries are taken care of. After which, I am sorry to say, you are to be placed under arrest.' He removed a revolver from under his jacket and trained it on Walt.

Seeing that Prescott was safely under control, Ben left him and ran to where Gemma was just stumbling to her feet. She threw herself into his arms.

'Ben, Ben, thank God you're here. I was so frightened,' she sobbed against his chest.

'It's okay,' he said, holding her close. 'No one's going to hurt you. Not ever again.' She tilted her head back and looked up at him through her tears.

'Take me home, please. Take me back to my father. I want to go home.'

'And Marianne?'

'She's . . . lost. They all are,' Gemma said, sobbing. 'I'll ask my father to help them, get them home, get treatment for them, even, if they're willing. I tried to persuade Marianne to come with me when I left, but she was too far gone to respond to friendship, or to much of anything. That's the real crime those men committed, destroying those young lives.'

'It might still be possible to help them. I'm glad you didn't give in yourself.'

A police car had arrived, and the officers were escorting Walt Prescott to it. Ben took Gemma's arm.

'Let's get you away from here,' he said. 'We'll have a lot to talk about on the way back home. There are things I haven't told you which you need to know, if you think you might like to take a chance on me.'

'I think,' she said, 'I know everything I need to know.' She added, 'And I'm thankful for that.'

We do hope that you have enjoyed reading this large print book.

Did you know that all of our titles are available for purchase?

We publish a wide range of high quality large print books including:
Romances, Mysteries, Classics
General Fiction
Non Fiction and Westerns

Special interest titles available in large print are:
The Little Oxford Dictionary
Music Book, Song Book
Hymn Book, Service Book

Also available from us courtesy of Oxford University Press:
Young Readers' Dictionary
(large print edition)
Young Readers' Thesaurus
(large print edition)

For further information or a free brochure, please contact us at:
Ulverscroft Large Print Books Ltd.,
The Green, Bradgate Road, Anstey,
Leicester, LE7 7FU, England.
Tel: (00 44) **0116 236 4325**
Fax: (00 44) **0116 234 0205**

Other titles in the
Linford Mystery Library:

SHERLOCK HOLMES: THE FOUR-HANDED GAME

Paul D. Gilbert

Holmes and Watson find themselves bombarded with an avalanche of dramatic cases! Holmes enrols Inspectors Lestrade and Bradstreet to help him play a dangerous four-handed game against an organization whose power and influence seems to know no bounds. As dissimilar as the cases seem to be — robbery, assault, and gruesome murder — Holmes suspects that each one has been meticulously designed to lure him towards a conclusion that even he could not have anticipated. However, when his brother Mycroft goes missing, he realises that he is running out of time . . .

THE MANUSCRIPT KILLER

Noel Lee

When Detective Inspector Drizzle receives a mysterious message from elderly recluse Matthew Trevelyn imploring him to visit the next day, as he is in fear of his life, Drizzle sets out straight away. Delayed by a punctured tyre, however, he arrives at the country house to discover he's too late: Trevelyn has been brutally murdered — strangled by a silk scarf belonging to his niece. Her boyfriend had been thrown out the previous night after a raging quarrel with Trevelyn — but is he the true culprit? Thus begins Drizzle's strangest case . . .

A HUNDRED THOUSAND REASONS FOR REVENGE

Edmund Glasby

Against a backdrop of Hollywood glamour, greed, betrayal and bizarre cults, a man is found dead in circumstances that defy explanation. Is it murder? An accident? Suicide? Or something else? FBI Special Agent Brett Dawson and unorthodox private investigator Vincent Stoker join forces to discover the truth. Following the grisly and perplexing leads from an unlikely start in small-town America through the mansions and dives of Los Angeles, their path takes them to a final showdown in the desert where they must put their faith in the unbelievable to survive.

THE RIVER MEN

Gerald Verner

Twenty-seven robberies, fifteen cargo broaches, and seven cases of murder: not in the past fifty years has there been such an outbreak of thieving and crime on the Thames; and in no single instance has the culprit been brought to justice, or his identity discovered. A new criminal organization with a mystery man at its head is playing the London river police for fools — and the latest officer on the case has been murdered, his body weighted and sunk in the river. Such is the challenge facing Inspector Terry Ward . . .

YOU CAN'T CATCH ME

Lawrence Lariar

Somewhat against his better judgment, Mike Wells accepts a lucrative assignment from bigtime gangster Rico Bruck. It seems a simple enough job: to board a train and shadow a man on his journey to New York, and then to telephone his whereabouts to Bruck. Mike takes with him the beautiful Toni Kaye, who tells him she wants to escape Bruck's employment and make a career as a singer. But when they arrive at their destination, their target is found murdered . . .